GERIATRICKS 1

GERIATRICKS 1

Henry's Brolly
Maddie's UXB
Tobias's Cattle
A Rotary Rendezvous
(a poem)

To Brian
Derek

Derek G Mynard

Copyright © 2013 Derek G Mynard
The moral right of the author has been asserted.

This book is a work of fiction. The characters, incidents, and dialogue are drawn from the author's imagination and are not to be construed as real. Any resemblance to persons, living or dead, is entirely coincidental.

Apart from any fair dealing for the purposes of research or private study, or criticism or review, as permitted under the Copyright, Designs and Patents Act 1988, this publication may only be reproduced, stored or transmitted, in any form or by any means, with the prior permission in writing of the publishers, or in the case of reprographic reproduction in accordance with the terms of licences issued by the Copyright Licensing Agency. Enquiries concerning reproduction outside those terms should be sent to the publishers.

Matador
9 Priory Business Park
Kibworth Beauchamp
Leicestershire LE8 0RX, UK
Tel: (+44) 116 279 2299
Fax: (+44) 116 279 2277
Email: books@troubador.co.uk
Web: www.troubador.co.uk/matador

ISBN 978 1783061 709

British Library Cataloguing in Publication Data.
A catalogue record for this book is available from the British Library.

Typeset in Minion Pro by Troubador Publishing Ltd
Printed and bound in the UK by TJ International, Padstow, Cornwall

Matador is an imprint of Troubador Publishing Ltd

Dedicated to my very good friends Brian and Geoffrey who had the patience and expertise to right my wrongs. Thank you.

CONTENTS

Introduction	ix
Henry's Brolly	1
Maddie's UXB	109
Tobias' Cattle	147
A Rotary Rendezvous	217

GERIATRICKS 1

Old Folk? Old folk, wearing tartan slippers, trammelled into the backwater of a comfy armchair in front of the tele? "Sit down Grandma, I'll get you a nice cup of cocoa". Oh yes, this is the lot of many geriatrics these days. When these out-of-sight 'oldies' do grope for a cane to stand up on shaky legs and open their mouths, they are perceived as cantankerous, rude, gossipy and out-of-date: "Have another biscuit Grandpa."

Born in times of war and adversity, these humble oldies remain canny, experienced and brave. They are especially 'up for it' when confronted with challenges, problems or oppression that could seriously affect their ways of life, bring about financial difficulties, interfere with a colleagues' welfare, even to destroy hard-earned reputations.

Geriatricks 1 has a cast of doughty, eccentric and humourous oldie characters who will just not 'stay out of sight and sit quietly'. Geriatricks unfolds as a series of novellas and poetry that will transport you into a world where 'old 'uns' address or answer their call to duty! Will their devilish plots, ploys and whirlwind fightbacks confound, bemuse to eventually lead to the defeat of their adversaries, and bring about victory – or not?

HENRY'S BROLLY

WARDLEY OFFICERS' RESIDENTIAL HOME

Located on the south coast of England at Plymington-next-the-Sea, this residential home is for elderly ex-officers, and their spouses, from the British armed forces, who wish to enjoy an active lifestyle in their retirement. Residents must be financially self sufficient, relatively mobile and participate in most of the home's activities.

Staffing levels at this residential home have, however, steadily increased over the last three years in order to cope with an increase of residents – to the maximum number permitted. Of necessity, this has led to a steady escalation of the residents' monthly maintenance bills. To combat this, a coterie of residents formed a 'breakfast volunteer group', where the breakfast serving service would be undertaken by them, thus allowing management to 'release' several table waiting staff, with the desired result of easing the residents' maintenance bills.

The forming of a breakfast volunteer group was not favoured by certain of the senior staff at the home and the situation has become acrimonious, leading to disputes and arguments. Steadfastly, the breakfast volunteer group continue to undertake their unaccustomed culinary duties with zeal, humour and a certain 'thumbing of the nose' at those who opposed the forming of such a group.

Their main antagonist, 'anti-oldie' Superintendant, Moira Sixpenny, seeks every opportunity to have the 'breakfast' situation reversed, and is determined to find a way, any way, to achieve this …

Geriatricks 1

Retired now – their military service honourably done,
Comfortable, tranquil? Oh, ho! Let us have some fun,
But Wardley's residents home economics now dictate,
All together now: a breakfast squad they must create,
Superintendent Sixpenny does oppose this campaign,
Infighting ensues to challenge her long, mighty reign,
Ah! Then Henry's brolly appears to tarnish the scene,
Yeah! Whoopee! Super Sixpenny's face is now abeam.

"Where on earth is everybody this morning?" moans Millicent Havers, hands on hips surveying the buffet breakfast table, laid out with shiny, hot metal trays containing the morning's offering, sizzling bacon; eggs, fried and scrambled; chunky farm sausages; baked-beans; fried tomatoes, mushrooms, black pudding, a variety of cereal and porridge; tinned and fresh fruit; fruit juices; jugs of milk and a large hot water urn for coffee or tea. "We are going to be terribly short-handed," says Millicent, spreading her arms wide, appealing to Belinda Huxley and Joe Baker, Capt. RN Rtd., both of them busy, preparing to serve a crowd of elderly, impatient, chattering, hungry residents gathered at the doorway of the dining room. The two shrug, shaking their heads.

"Mornin' t'ye all," booms Roger Marshall, Col. RE Rtd., striding into the dining room from a side door and slapping his right thigh with a rolled-up *Times* emphasising his presence. He sniffs as he takes up his position at the breakfast table behind the bacon and sausages. "My God, this lot smells good enough to eat."

"And a good morning to you, too," ventures Joe, waving a hand to waft away the steam.

"You are late, Roger. And both Henry and Rosemary are not here yet," complains Millicent.

A minor cyclone storms into the buffet area, "And where the heck is Henry Osbourne this morning? I do not see him at his station," roars Rosemary Carter-Smythe, the self-imposed doyen of the breakfast volunteer group. She glowers as she is ignored by those who, all of a sudden, become engaged with their preparations for the inrush of elderly residents.

"Somewhat unusual for Henry not to be working the toaster," says Roger. He sighs as he looks down at the bubbling pile of streaky bacon, bulging juicy sausages, succulent meat balls and black pudding. He takes up and click-clacks a pair of serving tongs. "Action stations, what!"

"Perhaps Henry is unwell?" Millicent suggests, as she looks at the wall clock and then beckons to the patiently waiting residents to move forward. In seconds withered, grasping hands pick up, wave, bang and slide trays onto the chrome guide-rails, with the usual elbow-battle to be first in the queue.

"Nope," states Roger, "Henry is not unwell; leastwise not here at the home. Superintendent Sixpenny just grabbed of my arm as I was passing, er, dashing here to do my duty. I thought at first she was being frisky, heh, heh! Instead she confided in me that Henry did not, I repeat, did not return to the home last night. Did I know anything about him? How's that for breaking news!"

"So Henwy stayed in town overnight," suggests Joe, raising bushy eyebrows, "Intewesting."

"Apparently, Super said, he signed out at three yesterday afternoon to go shopping, togged up as usual in his Savile Row suit and bowler and toting that brolly of his. Never to be seen again by all accounts."

"Don't be so dramatic," says Belinda, testing the heat of the big water urn with the back of her hand. "Mind, I did notice his absence at dinner last night; although that's not unusual for Henry as he often visits one or another of his Rotary pals in town for a round of bridge, a chat and a tot or two. But he's usually back for ten-thirty." She splashes ice-cooled orange juice from a jug into a row of glasses in readiness to hand out. "It's possible he imbibed a tot too many. Hmm; perhaps invited to sleep over?"

"Toast please, Millicent dearest," quavers an ancient female. Her gnarled hand hovering as she scans the spread in an exaggerated manner. "Oh dear, where is the toast? The normal place is quite empty."

"So it is, my dear," says Millicent loudly to the lady she knows to be hard of hearing. "It's Henry. It's his task to look after the toast, but because he is not here this morning, no toast!"

Roger gives a deep groan: "Ye know, after so much tutoring and so many hours spent at the toaster showing the chappie how to set the machine to produce toast just the right colour and crispness; to think we gave him the title of toastmaster after a mere six weeks of training. Hah! Gratitude!"

"A severe reprimand in coming Henry's way I'm telling you," growls Rosemary. "He's for the proverbial high jump. Washing up in the kitchen for a fortnight. Hah!"

"Move aside, I'll come round, and I'll have a go," says Stanley Donovan, Maj, R.A. Rtd. He leaves the queue and squeezes between a rather large Rosemary and a rear table, upon which the automatic toaster is located. He sidles into position. "You people are quite hopeless, it seems you are able to do only one thing at a time, you poor, poor souls."

"Can't agwee there m'dear fellow. It's just that each of us has a specific task at the bweakfast-fest. Dear old Henry is Toastmaster, I'm bacon, sausages and those meatball things; Miwicent eggs, scrambled, fried or omletted. Rosemary doles out the messy stuff: tomatoes, baked beans, mushrooms and Roger is fwesh fwuit and Bewinda takes care of the liquids: milk, juices, coffee and tea. Kippers are a special order. Now, what t'was it you were saying m'dear fellow. Hopeless?"

Stanley grimaces at Joe's detailed reprimand. He places several slices of wholemeal bread on the rack of the toaster rack and pokes a green button and watches as, inch-by-inch, the slices are drawn into the glowing interior of the machine. "I suppose I ought to become more involved after just hearing how one person's absence can cause so much of a problem."

"Ye seem conversant wi' that toasting machine Stanley Donovan," observes Roger Marshall.

"I was a Major in the Royal Artillery; expert on heat-seeking missiles," retorts Stanley, straight-faced.

"He babbles here, he babbles there, he babbles everywhere," crows Belinda, as she carefully turns the urn's tap to fill a teapot with hot water. "We're all agog as to why dear Henry is absent, but all you do Joe Baker, is cock-a-doodle-doo over who's assigned to undertake what task at the breakfast buffet."

Growing in number, members of the retired officers' residential home shuffle and hobble in an orderly manner along the front of the laden buffet spread, grasping trays, pausing at each section where self-designated savants ladle, spoon or place their respective offerings on plates with ingratiating smiles, apt comments, usually about the weather prospects for the morning's bowls session on the terrace, last night's television crime shock denouement or exchange, with knowing grins, winks and nose-taps of the latest gossip.

"Well. I for one am worried about Henry's whereabouts. It's not like him to miss his breakfast duty," says Millicent. "Stanley, please mind the eggs while I go and speak to Superintendant Sixpenny."

Stanley smiles, nodding. Millicent smooths her patterned pinafore and inches her slight figure behind those serving to make for the door leading to the reception and office areas.

"He's run away, that's what," broadcasts Rosemary, spooning lumpy tomatoes onto a plate.

"What was that?" enquires Roger, adjusting his ear-piece.

"Vamoosed," she shouts. "Gone orf."

"Ah! It's probably his past catching up with him. Secret service and all that," joins Roger. "KGB, Stasi, CIA, whomever. Bound to be one of that lot involved."

"Spwooks are forever spwooks," joins Joe, "It's in their blood, you know."

"Probably being held to ransom by one of them I should'na wonder. What he's worth? A million?"

"Don't be ridiculous," retorts Rosemary, "You've been reading too many James Bond novels. I think it's the pressure of being here at seven o'clock on the dot every morning, toiling away at a hot toaster–"

"She's got a crush on him, you know," says Belinda.
"Who has?" asks Joe.
"Milly Havers," Belinda says in a hushed voice.
"On whom?" asks Rosemary.
"Henry Osbourne of course."
"The man's over eighty for God's sake," retorts Rosemary, "and as bald as a coot."
"So what? Just because the fellah's beached, ready for the breaker's yard and has a shiny pate, does'na mean he's beyond enjoying a wee bit of romance in later life," argues Roger.
"No passion, no allure, no fun," says Rosemary, sniffing.
"Not by any stretch of the imagination can I imagine Miwicent and Henwy being entwined together," says Joe, with a raised eyebrow.
"Been walking round with your eyes closed? Haven't ye seen him blowing kisses at the lady, almost at every meal-time and in the common lounge, and… having wine delivered to her table?" says Roger
"I have seen him behaving oddly of late. Thought he looked tired, had a list to port last time– "
"Port? Too early for port. Mind… hang on," Roger puts hand to ear. "Ye mentioned port?"
"… I saw him, he yawns a lot and blowing kisses is a sign of being out of puff?" agrees Joe.
"Out of puff? I suppose that astute observation is to be expected from the assistant Captain of Racing at the Royal Plymington Yacht Club!"
"I wesent that comment," retorts Joe. "I was merely–"

"Look, you're running low on sausages, buzz Chef before we have a mini riot on our hands," says Roger.

"Over sausages?" queries Stanley, turning from the toaster.

"Ye'd be surprised. Chanting, waving napkins, knives and forks, tapping wine glasses, breathing fire and brimstone. Real active protesters this lot can be, 'specially when they get their dander up. Ye'll see when you have been here a while longer." Roger accentuates with a wave of his serving tongs

"I'll buzz the Chef," says Joe.

Millicent returns to the breakfast room after some fifteen minutes; she resumes her position.

"News of Henry, Milly?" queries Joe as he moves to press the kitchen staff's alert buzzer.

She gives him a meaningful look, "Super Sixpenny tells me she's going to have to contact the police. She has phoned several of his known friends in town, but with no luck; there is no sign of him anywhere in the home or the common rooms. So she tells me she'll have to designate Henry as a missing person if there's no news of him by half-past-nine."

"Speak up Milly," says Roger, keen to hear.

"Designate Henry as a missing person," says Millicent, louder.

"Designate? That sounds awfully official. What does that entail?"

"First, to inform the police and let them know one of our souls is missing."

"Bit drastic, what?" says Roger.

"I'm sure there is a perfectly logical explanation.

Henry is quite level-headed, he's nobody's fool. After all, he was in military intelligence, MI5, you know." Milicent looks proudly around.

"Always going on about it. Ye'd think he won the cold war single-handed," groans Roger.

"He is no show-off," Millicent retorts, "he is a quiet, kindly man."

"Secondly?" urges Stanley.

"Those closest to him will have to give an account of his latest movements and, er, probably ask about his state of mind, from whomever was last with him," says Millicent.

"That's sounds like a problem," says Stanley, "getting information from those who aren't qualified."

"Oh, I don't think it's anything more serious than getting to the bottom of where he is," says Millicent.

The two lapse into silence while Roger, Belinda, Joe and Rosemary, continue doling out food and drink to an ever-growing number of chattering, hunger-driven ancients.

"When I get my hands on that Henry, well… he'll be toast all right!" barks Rosemary.

"You heard that Millicent learned from the Superintendent that Henry is A.W.O.L," interrupts Roger.

"What do you mean, A.W.O.L?" Rosemary asks, as she casts a sidelong glance to judge the number of residents filing past, pushing their trays along the rails.

"Absent Without Leave," states Belinda.

"Stop pretending ye don't know military lingo m'dear. Demeans you," jeers Roger, unwisely trying to grip a slippery peach slice with his tongs to eventually flop it onto a proffered, shaking bowl. "And you hitched to a Colonel for umpteen years."

"Stuff and nonsense. Anyway, where is he A.W.O.L at?" barks Rosemary.

"If we knew that he wouldn't be A.W.O.L would he?"

A deep sigh erupts from Rosemary. "So, what's to happen about Henry Osbourne being, er, A.W.O.L?"

"Milly says Super told her she'll have to report him missing to the police. House wules," says Joe.

"Ha! Missing persons alert. Last time we lost one of our number we found out she was busy getting herself drowned in the briny. Brilliant, warm, sunny day it was when Molly Sinclaire, after a pint of cider, decided she would go a-paddling on one of those surfboard thingamajigs. Seventy-eight, thought she was thirty-five. She fell, slid, off the thing half a mile from the shore. Curtains! Hell of a kerfuffle. The rescue chopper quickly enough raised her up to that watery haven in the sky. Oodles of grub and bubbly at her wake, a real spirited affair; her old man, Eddy, played a sea shanty on his ukulele: What shall we do with a drunken sailor? Hah! Most of us got quite tipsy."

"I don't think Henry would get into any unsavoury go-ings on," says Millicent quietly.

"Wouldn't call getting drowned unsavoury m'dear. Jest bloody careless," snorts Rosemary.

"This recent?" inquires Stanley.

"Nay, t'was a year ago," says Roger. "Then there was old Tobias Cox, bashed his skull, killed him stone dead," reminisces Roger.

"A perpetrator?" queries Stanley.

"Nay, he was sliding down the bannister in Dulverton block, fell off half way down. Splat!"

"That is enough, Roger. Tobias was a dear old soul and we miss him."

"Sinister bunch, these Secret Service types. Can't tell what they get up to," says Rosemary. "Meanwhile, I see you rounded up Stanley here as Henry's stand-in to work the toaster?"

"He volunteered actually–" starts Joe.

"Goodness, gracious me. A volunteer! Took me six months to convince you reprobates we must serve breakfast ourselves to save on staff salaries, to cut back on the outrageous charges the home puts–"

"Much to the annoyance of our most beloved Tanner," interrupts Joe.

"Tanner?" queries Stanley.

"With a name like Sixpenny, what else?" retorts Belinda.

"Our pet name for her, dahling," purrs Rosemary.

"I see. But, why would she be annoyed?" asks Stanley.

"We pressured Tanner and her admin cohorts to get our monthly charges reduced to a reasonable level because we felt staffing costs were well over the top and could be reduced. She was thus pressured to call a management-residents' meeting to hear our idea as to how this may be achieved."

"But only after we petitioned all of the residents," joins Millicent, "to force the issue."

"Hey-up, owange juice needs topping-up Belinda," growls Joe.

"When Tanner finally convened a meeting, she had the audacity to suggest that such a privileged well-to-do bunch of OAPs such as ourselves – we need more mashed, bashed and fried, Milly – could not only afford the staffing levels, but servants as well, if we were so minded," recounts a riled Rosemary.

"Hah! We should be so wucky," says Joe.

"Then, she had the temerity, after my opener to the floor, to call me "hoity-toity", would you believe. I almost kicked the dear lady up her obnoxious arse," says Rosemary, with a beligerent glare.

"Rosemary, language, language," rebukes Millicent.

"There'll be a lot more of it if we don't jolly-up these old-timers from their morning sleep-walk, we're near to closing time. We'll give 'em another fifteen minutes, then we'll prepare the room-specials."

"So what happened next," presses Stanley, "at the resident's meeting?"

"Well, we got precisely nowhere. Tanner and Dudley Fortescue, Chairman of the Board, downplayed our concerns, prevaricated, argued the impracticability of our proposal, blocking our every move, then they guillotined the meeting. Afterwards we studied our contracts and found, with Belinda's help – she was a lawyer in the Army – that a two-third majority of residents could enforce, modify or change any situation considered unfavourable to residents. So we obtained the Home's accounts, and studied staff salaries and perks. We determined savings could be made, we lobbied all residents and called an emergency meeting. There we elected to do away with breakfast table waiting and instead run a buffet service. This we would undertake ourselves, those who were capable, that is. After all is said and done we, none of us, were doing anything at that time of the morning, except watch replay golf tounaments on the telly. Upshot: we would release three serving staff and save several thousands of pounds a year, the equivalent of one month's payment for most of us." Rosemary, momentarily losing focus on the food situation adds, "where are we?"

"But... we do have table service, at evening dining?" appeals Stanley.

"My dear fellow, we are talking bwekkers?" says Joe, "We couldn't stwetch ourselves to do a dinner; too, too much to expect of a few wolunteers, to stuff those fancy napkins in those fancy wings, wait on table all dwessed up. At least a two hour stint. No, a buffet evening dinner wasn't on the cards. Anyway, there would have been a huge outcry from our own people, never mind management. But doing a bweakfast buffet is pwactical, it saves money, and we have reduced our monthly maintenance bill by fifteen percent."

"How did this affect relationships with the managment?" asks Stanley.

"Moira Sixpenny, Tanner, and Dudley Fortescue didn't like it one bit, especially because the trustees at large, by now a very unhappy bunch, took them to task because they'd allowed the situation to get to that stage. Less money for them to dole out in bonuses and such," say Belinda.

"What really put their noses further out of joint was the suggestion we do the same with the bar. There are only two staffing it, and by limiting the opening hours somewhat, we could manage that," says Roger.

"Tanner saw all this as an attack on her reign supreme hence her relentless pursuance in trying to concoct, machinate, any reason to get us, the breakfast squad, disbanded, even dishonoured. The lady hates dogs, canaries and independent oldies." Rosemary is virtually gnashing her teeth.

"One wonders why she is Superintendent of a retirement home. If she make no hiding the fact that she is so much against elderly people."

"Hah! You're not the only one to ask that question."

"Well… her credentials are impeccable," boasts Stanley, "I've sighted the lady's CV."

"You! How's that, since you've only been here a short time?" queries Belinda.

"Erm," Stanley hesitates, "Must have been during my initial interview, to become resident here."

"That's strange. Moira plays her cards close to her, er um, chest as it were. She's that sort you know?"

"I think she is a thoroughly decent, trustworthy woman," insists Stanley. "I found her so anyway."

"Ye're rather familiar with the lady," suggests Roger.

"I say. You espied her CV, eh?" interrupts Rosemary. "More than most of us… anything juicy?"

"She has been very kind to me. My interview was absolutely straightforward." Stanley straightens up.

"She's a bully, obnoxious, and with those who canna to stand up to her, spiteful," barks Roger. "She is quality all right, with a capital K."

"So is her dogsbody, that Samantha Meadows. A swawny, cweepy cweature, that one," says Joe.

"We'll yet unearth some dirty linen, find some reason to get Tanner on her bike," murmurs Rosemary.

"Yes, we must continue to explore ways and means," agrees Belinda.

"Hey-up, eggs, fried and scrambled, now, press the Chef's buzzer," advises Roger.

"Don't bother, there's only a few left to serve," says Millicent. "We'll have enough."

They idly chat as they tend to the thinning queue with their relatively new-found culinary skills.

"Nine-thirty. Time to shut up shop," barks Rosemary. "Milly, I think you've got the room-specials list?"

"Yes. Six poor souls this morning calling for breakfast in their rooms. We'll prepare them just now."

"I shall be launching an enquiry as to why Henry is absent from his breakfast duties," says Rosemary,

"Don't be so melodwamatic Wosemary. He'd not miss his duty without good cause," says Joe.

"Won't wash with me. We set up this arrangement to save money, but it does need all of us to pull our weight for it to be a success. By the way, thank you for helping out this morning Stanley."

Stanley simpers and nods.

"That's all of the walking residents gone through," observes Roger. "I'll buzz the kitchen staff to tell 'em we've finished out here; we'll send someone to collect and deliver the room-specials."

"You're avoiding my suggestion we hold an inquiry over Henry," dictates Rosemary.

"Rosemary, drop the polemic. Let's go and sit down and have our own breakfasts?" encourages Millicent.

"All right, all right. I'll bring the coffees over," agrees Rosemary.

"And Stanle-e-e-e-y, I'll have four slices of toast and marmalade," quips Roger.

Stanley his forehead furrowed, repacking bread slices into bags, says: "Excuse me, I have to, er, make a call. I'll be back as soon as I can." He folds the bread bags a sidles from behind the serving area.

One-by-one the breakfast team saunter over to the sitting area, three of them carrying piled-up, breakfast plates. They head to one side, clear of the fifty-odd munching, chattering, dribbling, newspaper-reading residents. They gather round a vacated table with seating for six.

"Ha! An O group, what!" barks Roger, slumping down on a chair.

A sigh from Rosemary, "An O group?"

"A what-to-do-next meeting," he replies, grinning. "Needed 'em all the time in bomb disposal."

"Why am I not one bit surprised at that, if you were running the show," Rosemary retorts.

"Well, I don't know what we can do about Henry. We shall have to be patient and hope the authorities, here at the home and the police, carry out their checks efficiently and find him a.s.a.p," says Belinda.

Rosemary wobbles over, balancing a tray of mugs of coffee and milk. She sets the tray down saying, "Surely Tanner and that Samantha girl ought to have been around to each of us by now asking about Henry's last movements. Interviewing we who are closest to him?" She eases herself down onto a chair.

"My, quite the organiser, aren't we?" smiles Belinda, forking a slice of sausage into her mouth.

"You're right. Neither she, nor any of the staff, have been round to ask about our Henry," says Joe.

"Early days yet," says Belinda.

They eat, sip coffee, rest chins on elbows and become lost in their own thoughts. Roger folds his *Times* to the crossword puzzle page, studies the clues and frowns. "Four down... ye Gods!" He gropes for the biro in his shirt pocket, uttering, "Poseidon."

"You do not really think the pwessure of Henry being toastmaster caused him to up sticks?" asks Joe.

"Don't be silly," says Rosemary, "Keen as mustard helping to save money by doing breakfast, I suppose if anything his is the easier task, feeding slices of bread into an automatic toaster, hardly arduous. You saw how easily Stanley coped. If he can do it at the drop of a hat, almost anyone can do it."

"Takes skill getting the colour just right," adds Belinda. "And what's Poseidon got to do with anything?"

"The clue m'dear, the clue: 'A hairy, three-way fishy tail. Eight letters'," responds Roger, smiling.

"Please don't go on any more about the colour of toast," pleads Millicent.

"We'll organise a search of the out-buildings, by gosh," says an enthused Joe. "Maybe he nipped out for a touch of fwesh air in the night and twod on a garden rake, clobbered himself? Out sparkus, out there."

"Good idea. We'll round up the troops later," says Belinda. "Roger, how on Earth do you get Poseidon from a three-way fishy tale?"

"I wonder where Stanley has got to?" enquires Millicent.

"Gone orf somewhere," rasps Rosemary. "Darned fellow's always vanishing into the wide blue yonder."

"Has the fellow got memory problems, alzheimers, dementia? Does he wobble about?" asks Roger.

"No, Stanley always seems to have somewhere to go; no weaving, tottering, shaking or wobbling. Really, I have no idea where he goes," says Belinda vaguely. "But not usually to his room… I happen to know."

"Your internal spy system at work, eh?" grins Roger.

"I do not spy," Belinda retorts.

"Not 'how on Earth' m'dear," interrupts Roger, "Neptune is the key to Poseidon."

"I do not understand," says Belinda wearily, waving a floppy hand at Roger's reply.

"I think he's a cunning little weasel myself," murmurs Rosemary.

"Neptune?"

"No, Stanley."

"Why d'ye think that?" asks Roger.

"Gut feeling. How does a relative newcomer know so much about Tanner, and… one who says he has sighted her CV. Beats me," says Rosemary.

"It's no secret he spends lots of time in Tanner's office, drinking coffee."

"Neptune is the Roman God of the Sea, see," explains Roger. "He sports a beard, has a fish's tail and he grasps a trident. Hence: A hairy three-way fishy tail. Poseidon is the Greek name for Neptune."

"Mumbo jumbo if you ask me," complains a now bored Rosemary.

"You are all over-reacting," says Millicent. "Stanley's just finding his feet. This is a new environment for him. You must remember how difficult it was for us too, at first."

"Talk of the devil," murmurs Rosemary, as Stanley appears, looking round. He walks over to the group.

"Now then," announces Roger loudly, "what d'you know about Poseidon, Stanley?"

"It was a submarine-launched ballistic missile system introduced in 1971," Stanley boldly proclaims.

"Ask a ruddy simple question–" exclaims Roger.

"No cross words now." Rosemary says obliquely. "Anyway, I always thought Neptune was a planet."

"Neptune is the eighth and farthest planet from the Sun in the Solar System. It's the fourth-largest by diameter and the third-largest by mass. So my university tutor instilled upon our weary brains," Belinda says, a broad smile lighting up her stern countenance.

"I can't stand any more of this. What are we going to do about our missing Henry?" pleads Millicent.

"We should telephone all his friends for a start," suggests Joe.

"You're a bunch of geriatric no-brainers," sneers Rosemary. "It's no more than that the man found himself in a drunken stupor and he's sleeping it orf at one of his pal's places in town. There again, perhaps he's shacked up with some tart."

"Oh, Rosemary, you can be so crude. Henry would never do anything like that," protests Millicent.

"He's tall, he's elegant, he's handsome; maybe wealthy. In other words, he'd be quite a catch."

"You said earlier he was beached and balding…"

"Hush now, it was Roger who said…"

"No, it wasn't, it was you. Maybe he snuffed it?"

"We'd have heard by now if he had."

"Maybe lost his wallet? Or had it stolen?"

"What has his wallet got to do with it?"

"No wallet, no money. No wallet, no cards. No wallet, no taxi."

"He has his own motor, a nice little Smart car. Why wouldn't he drive home in that?" asks Rosemary.

"If he was a little tipsy he wouldn't drive. He's too sensible," says Millicent.

"I still think he's holed up in some posh hotel with a floozy. He likes blondes," grins Rosemary.

"Ye've forgotten to take your pills again m'dear, haven't you?" says Roger.

"Why do you say that?" Rosemary asks, frowning. "What's that got–"

"It's the way your eyes hooded when you said floozy, 'gives you a certain sex appeal," Roger raises and slowly unfurls his right palm, blowing Rosemary a kiss.

Rosemary colours up, and shakes her head. "Rubbish. I'm always alert and ready for the day ahead. And I do not appreciate your innuendo. I'm a decent–"

"I want ye to sweep me orf me feet," says Roger crudely, grinning, spreading his arms. "Phwoar!"

She glares at him. "That may well happen, but not the way you imagine, Roger Marshall."

"You should be taking those Omega 3 fish-oil capsules like I do. The big ones."

"Why?"

"Energy, brain-power, all sorts of reasons... sex for one."

"Brain power? You! There's a misnomer if ever I heard one. And as for sex, don't make me laugh."

"I reeemembeeer Poseeeeidon," sings Roger, reminding Rosemary of his superior brain-power.

"I imagine they'll have already checked Henry's room and other obvious places," Stanley suggests.

"Well, we can't just sit awound doing nothing," says Joe Baker.

"He's such a lovely, harmless man," murmurs Millicent.

"Ex-MI5, harmless! Don't believe it," says Rosemary.

"Does he have any welatives?" asks Joe.

"Brother died last year. Nobody else I know of," replies Millicent.

"Does he have a mobile phone?" queries Roger.

"I can't imagine an MI5 agent, even a long retired one, not having a mobile phone," says Belinda.

"Yes, he does have one," says Millicent.

"Has anybody tried calling him?"

"Yes, I have, three times. It seems to be turned off, I think," she replies.

They talk, lapse, talk and lapse, encouraging Roger's further crossword efforts with misleading and outlandish suggestions for almost an hour. Outside low

Henry's Brolly

clouds presage a period of drizzly rain and poor visibility. The mood is contagious, they sit glumly before their now-empty cold mugs, discarded plates and a rumpled, discarded newspaper.

Walter Masters clatters into the breakfast room at near ten-thirty with his trolley. He casts a wary eye over the casually seated breakfast crew, the empty plates, screwed-up napkins and coffee mugs. "You lot finished then?" he growls. "Not got the gyps from them farm sausages 'ave you?"

"No. One of our number is missing, Walter. We're waiting for news of his whereabouts," says Belinda.

"Dunno if its about 'im, but there was two coppers in reception askin' to see the superintendent when I come past just now." Walter gathers up the soiled mugs, plates and cutlery and places them on his trolley. "I saw Simple Samantha showin' them into her office. Oh! I mean Super's assistant," he corrects himself.

"Probably one of us having been caught yet again, speeding through Plymington's leafy environs," says Roger, wielding an imaginary steering wheel.

"They will have to raise the speed limit for the benefit of those of us who venture forth from Wardley Residential Home in ancient Rolls and zippy mobility scooters," says Belinda.

"It's a jungle out there these days," sighs Rosemary.

"Between us, by God, we must be financing the whole of the town's police force in traffic violation fines," chirps Roger.

"Pwerhaps their visit is to do with Henry," suggests Joe.

"Well, we ought go and find out," says Millicent, rising to her feet.

They take off their multi-coloured pinafores and file out of the dining room.

* * *

The breakfast squad, their morale boosted with the prospect of news about Henry, troop chattering into the reception area. Rosemary angles her head at Irene, the young blonde receptionist, this morning sporting a silk print blouse, large hoop earrings, and a face made up with fiery red lip-gloss. Irene casts wary blue eyes on the trouble-making gaggle standing before her.

"Superintendent Sixpenny free?" Rosemary barks, frowning at the sight of this young pretty soul in their midst. Who the devil hired such a lovely young creature? She, being Chair of the Resident's Committee, has no recollection of interviewing such a beauty. She'd bet a brass ha'penny it was Dudley Fortescue Senior, the Chairman of the Board of Trustees, foxy, sexy sod that he is, who elected to…

"I am afraid not, Miss Carter-Smythe. She has visitors with her," says Irene diplomatically. "And a good morning to you all."

"Who," growls in Roger, "is the esteemed Sixpenny engaging with?"

"I really can't say, sir," the young lady replies.

"Why?" asks Millicent.

"I must adhere to the rules, Madam," Irene says quietly, her lip gloss glowing under the neons.

"I would've thought two cwoppers in uniform obvious enough to tell us about," says Joe.

"Shut up Joe. You know damned well Sixpenny has the staff under her thumb," growls Rosemary.

"Miss Carter-Smythe, please!" protests Irene.

"Don't Miss me, Miss. I am Mrs to you. Goddit?" rasps Rosemary, resting her sizeable bosom on the reception desk.

"Yes, Madam," says Irene, politely angling her head.

"Oh, I give up," explodes an exasperated Rosemary, backing off, shucking her breasts to be comfortable.

"We really need to ask if there is any news about Henry Osbourne," asks Millicent pointedly.

"I must be discreet, Madam, but I will tell you that two police officers are in with with Superintendent Sixpenny, but I really don't know what it's about," says Irene, shuffling papers, hoping for an end to this endless interrogation by a bunch of nothing-better-to-do crappy oldies.

"Uniformed?" queries Belinda.

"As Mr Baker has already mentioned, Madam," responds Irene obliquely.

"A bold decision is called for, m'dears," says Rosemary, turning, appealing to the breakfast group.

"Agreed. We camp right here until we get some definite news about Henry," insists Roger.

"We don't know that the police offices are here about Henry, do we?" says Millicent.

"True, we don't. But there's damn-all to do until the weather improves and the bowling green dries out," says Roger. "So, let's give Tanner a worrysome moment or two."

Geriatricks 1

"Just for the hell of it," chuckles Joe.

"Here, here," adds Rosemary, with a wave towards the seating area.

Irene lowers her shapely self onto her seat, barely able to see over the desk, trying to keep an eye on this recalcitrant bunch. She sighs, dreaming fleetingly of her boyfriend shunting passengers in his minicab from Plymington's railway sation to the town's business hub and back again, and... when she will get to ride in the same cab herself at the end of her shift, to kiss him and ... she sighs and reaches for the internal phone to alert the Superintendent of the presence of the notorious, rebellious breakfast team outside her office.

The crew spread themselves about the reception area, sitting down on black leather armchairs and settees, hitching skirts, trousers and crossing legs. Roger exposes garish Argyle socks, Joe's showing white anchors on a blue background. Rosemary fiddles with her chiffon scarf. Belinda in beige trousers, knees apart, clasps her hands over her cane's knobbly handle. Millicent fidgets uncomfortably in an oversized patterned cardigan. They take in Irene, peering over the counter, otherwise they idly pass an eye over the domineering framed hanging picture of Field-Marshal Montgomery, with Rommel, his pet dog, and Winston Churchill. Two or three magazines are picked up, casually looked at and discarded. Rain splatters against the windows. Otherwise, silence...

Barely ten minutes pass when a ringtone playing the opening score of '633 Squadron' – in ninety-decibel blasts – shreds the silence asunder. The offended glare daggers at the source and visibly shudder with annoyance, others mouth-mime their complaint – all except Roger, "Attaboy," he roars, picking up on the theme tune. "Bravo, Millicent!"

An embarrassed Millicent gropes for her mobile, pulls it from her cardigan pocket, looking around as she presses a button and puzzled as to who could be calling her, not recognising the number on the screen.

"Hello?" she says cautiously.

"They're going to give me back my things," says a querulous voice.

She recognises it as Henry's. "Who will, Henry?" she waves at the others, pointing to her phone.

All eyes focus on Millicent, the noise impediment forgotten. Is this Henry?

"The police. I'm at the main Plymington Police Station," says Henry.

"Whatever for. What have you done?" pleads Milicent.

"Nothing."

"Have you been there all this time?" she asks.

"Yes, all night long."

"Why?"

"I was arrested yesterday afternoon at the supermarket. I've been in a police cell since then. They have finger-printed and photographed me."

"Why? How? What for?" is Millicent's urgent response.

"They are charging me with sexual molestation and resisting arrest."

"In a supermarket Henry? That's, that's awful." Millicent rolls her eyes.

"Yes it is. But I'm being released on police bail when the paperwork is complete."

"What can I, we, do?" she asks.

"Nothing at all. They say they will drive me back to the home in an hour or so."

"I must inform the others. We've all been so worried about you."

"That's a kind thing to say, Millicent."

"We have two policemen here as I speak. They're in with Tanner, er, Superintendent Sixpenny."

"Probably concerning myself, enquiring after my bona-fides. They just would not believe me here at the police station when I told them I was a retired MI5 officer living at Wardley."

"Do tell me what you have done, Henry?"

"Nothing. It's a terrible mix up."

"All right, we'll see you soon. Now I must tell the others that you are safe and you are coming home."

"Bye, Millicent."

"Bye, Henry." She slowly puts the mobile to sleep while raising her eyes to look at the others, their eyes focus on her. She announces, "I have located Henry."

"Where, for God's sake?" explodes Roger.

"Where the devil is the man?" barks Rosemary.

"Where?" asks Belinda.

"Where?" repeats Joe.

"At Plymington Police Station. He's been there all night… in a cell." Millicent verges on tears.

"Oh, ho! I smell trouble," says Belinda.

"Why was he in the clink?" queries Rosemary.

"What had he done?" interrupts Roger.

"He was arrested yesterday afternoon for some reason… at a supermarket," says Millicent.

"Why? What did he do? Nick some peppermints?"

"I don't know. He said he's being released on bail and will be driven back here in about an hour."

"Thunder and lightning, what fun," says Joe.

"Ye Gods," chortles Roger. "Not peppermints then?"

"Trust you to see this as a jolly old romp."

"Now look here my good lady!" starts Roger.

Then, they start to chuckle and smile. Henry is safe, our Henry is coming home.

Their joy is short-lived. Moira Sixpenny's door swings open. She emerges with two uniformed police officers at her shoulder. Sidekick Samantha hovers, peering round the door jam. The three look curiously at five pairs of raised, expectant eyes.

"I have been informed," starts Sixpenny, head held high, in a superior voice, "that Henry Osbourne has been in police custody since yesterday afternoon. He will be released later this morning. I cannot say any more at this time. There will be an official statement issued later on."

"They don't seem like the bunch of deviants reputation has it, do they? mutters tall, moustached, PC Willie Watkins to his fellow officer, taking the rise out of this band of creaking, senile oldies, eyeing them up and down.

"Can't always tell; only when they make it to a certain age does it begin to show," replies WPC Fanny Short out of the side of her mouth, playing the game. "But this lot look like they've already got there."

Roger tweaks his hearing aid. "Ah, ha," he barks,

standing up, "Should we apprehend these interlopers, fellow breakfasteers?" The two police officers halt mid-stride, looking askance at Roger. Sixpenny, with a deep sigh, hand-gestures Roger to move aside.

"These two mawcontents standing foursquare before us?" questions Joe, going alto.

"Yeah, it be they," bellows Rosemary, standing, diamond earrings flashing, her hefty bosom heaving.

"On what charge," belts out Joe, also rising to his feet, "shall we pwess upon these mawcontents?"

"Language, of course m'luds. Lousy language," utters Roger in a sonorous voice.

"So, what ails their language, I ask thee?" intones Belinda, swelling up, playing along, eyes a-twinkle.

Roger looks at Rosemary, then at the two police officers, saying in moderato, "The quality of their uttered word is mere mumble and jumble, such is not permitted in this revered establishment. The spoken word must be clear and concise, so that all may comprehend, understand, respond, react and bloody-well hear properly!"

"Shall we incarcerate these ne'er-do-wells, or let them pass with serious admonishment?"

"Slam 'em up in the nick. Elecution lessons, on the hour every hour,' barks a gleeful Rosemary

"Send 'em forthwith to the cells my dear colleagues, for they have wrought a serious wrong."

"No, we being benevolent cweatures, we ought let them pass... " says Joe, with a deep, sad mock sigh.

"With a wee caution that they improve their verbal ways. Aye, let 'em pass!" responds Roger.

"Then, fellow breakfasteers, step aside," booms Rosemary, stepping back with a mock bow, tossing her scarf over her shoulder and, with an imperious wave of her mighty arm, invites the two coppers to pass.

"Oooh," squeals Millicent, fluttering a delicate pink hanky.

The officers look round at the squad. "Say nowt," whispers the tall moustached one. "This lot are totally bonkers. Let's get out while we can. If they follow, the Taser's in the patrol car."

Sixpenny ushers the two officers with undue haste to the front swing-doors. "You must not be hasty in passing judgment," she says. "Some of our residents can, at times, be cantankerous, insubordinate and, er, unpredictable. They are really kindly souls at heart, all having served their country with honour and distinction over many, many years. However this, er, group, well... I do apologise if they seem to be–"

"We bid you good-day madam," says PC Watkins, backing through the swing-door, then swiveling to follow on behind his companion. The two flee the building at the double.

"You see, moustache almost touched his forelock," whispers Joe.

"Ah ha, you begin to see the light," says Rosemary.

"Which shinest only on the blessed," intones Roger.

Moira Sixpenny, en-route to her office, is shaking with fury. She stops, turning on Roger: "I don't think you know what you've done, Major Marshall."

"Pissed orf two coppers," he chuckles.

"We shall get a bad reputation–" Sixpenny starts.

"Far too late m'girl," says Rosemary, with a huge grin. Sixpenny throws her head back and stalks into her office.

* * *

A blue, yellow and silver check-adorned police car draws up at the front entrance of Wardley Officers' Residential home. The same two police officers, both now wearing a hi-vis jackets, athletically exit their car. WPC Short goes round to assist Henry as he unfolds and climbs stiffly out of the rear door, supporting him by the elbow to lead him through the home's swing-doors and into the reception area. PC Watkins follows, carrying Henry's two supermarket, emblazoned bags bulky with groceries, his bowler and a clipboard. They escort and deposit the dishevelled Henry at the desk.

Superintendent Sixpenny appears at her office door. She steps out and stands foursquare before Henry. Her face is grim, ankle-booted feet set apart, tan skirt taut at the knee, flared below, with her arms stiff by her sides in an affected posture as if to bar Henry's entry to the home. WPC Short releases Henry's arm and pauses for a few moments while PC Watkins places Henry's bowler and shopping bags on the desk, then he passes the clipboard with papers affixed over to the benign Irene, who glances at it and shaking her head, promptly passes it to Superintendent Sixpenny who gives her an icy glare as she reaches for the proffered board and pen. She too studies the paperwork and then, after a moments hesitation, signs the paper.

No words are spoken, loud or whispered by the two officers who promptly about turn and depart.

Sixpenny moves close, nose-to-nose, to address Henry, "Under the terms of your bail, Mr Osbourne, you are to remain at the home. You cannot leave it at any time until we receive further instruction from the police authorities. Although I expect you have been so advised already, hmm?"

Henry slowly removes his glasses. "We are in rather close proximity, Superintendent Sixpenny. So do be kind enough to back off. Now if you please!" The lady, sensing conflict in the offing, backs off as told. "I have heard and I understand the terms of my bail," Henry continues. "Also I am extremely tired since I've had very little sleep and there is a great deal for me to think about. So I shall retire to my room."

"Irene," barks Sixpenny. "Call Nurse Prestwick, now, and tell her to visit Mr Osbourne in his room. I will notify the staff as to Mr Osbourne's situation personally, and I will also inform the Chairman of the Board of Trustees at the earliest opportunity."

"With a great deal of discretion, I plead Superintendent," says Henry. "The situation, as you are wont to believe, may not be all that it seems. There is much yet to be addressed."

"I'll say there is! I realise there is a lot more to this incident than meets the eye. Hah! I should say so."

"Tread warily, Superintendent Sixpenny, I do advise," Henry replaces his glasses.

Super Sixpenny lets rip, "It will ruin Wardley's reputation if it gets to be known in the neighbourhood as a retirement home that houses sex perverts who assault young women in the town. Parents with grandchildren and relatives, will stop coming to visit our residents. The newspapers will have a field-day prying and photographing–"

"You are speaking in the abstract ma'am, I trust?" Henry interrupts, raising his eyebrows.

"I speak as I find," Sixpenny storms.

"Very unwise," says Henry.

"The Board of Trustees have it within their power to remove those who are found to be lawbreak–"

"Do be warned, Superintendent, I will take action if I perceive slander," he says with steel in his voice.

"You will what?"

"You understand me well enough. Now excuse me and good-day to you," Henry inclines his head at Irene and the others, walking out of the reception area carrying his bowler and the two shopping bags.

* * *

After lunch the breakfast crew gather in the communal lounge where the bar is still open, and busy.

"Ye know," says Roger, "our squad's bid to run the bar, in addition to the breakfast buffet, is coming up at the next management-residents' meeting–"

"It's not going to happen, Woger, unless we draw Tanner's teeth, neutralise the lady somehow," says Joe.

"Agreed, she is the main sticking point," says Roger, stroking his jaw thoughtfuly.

"Mind you, our projections in terms of savings might just swing it our way."

"Good God man, I can just see you and I shaking and stirring–" starts Joe.

"Did ye here the one about the Scottish crocodile serving drinks in a bar in Miami–"

"Enough idle chatter, you two reprobates," the voice of Rosemary Carter-Smythe cuts the air. "We have work to do, not engage in telling fairy stories."

"To do with running the bar, or the Miami joke?" enquires Roger, grinning.

Rosemary ignores this attempt to draw her out. "Sit," she orders. The three, joined by Henry, Belinda and Millicent, settle themselves one way or another into armchairs around a low table. Henry becomes the centre of focus having returned to their midst after being examined by the duty nurse, and having taken a short nap. Joe waves over a smart red-waistcoated barman and orders a bottle of Glenfiddich Single Malt and glasses. Henry commences to narrate the series of events that led to his arrest.

"You what!" bellows Joe.

"I do not believe it," shouts Rosemary.

"So, as I understand it, ye've been accused of sexually molesting a young lady in a supermarket with your BROLLY?" overstates Roger.

"My goodness," squeals Millicent, hand over mouth. "That's awful."

"Have a tot, Henry," suggests Roger. "Just to get yeself properly oriented." He stands up and splashes liberal quantities of scotch into two glasses, as well as his own and Henry's. He passes the bottle in front of Millicent's eyes, she shakes her head.

They look up as Stanley walks in. Roger shrugs as Belinda waves to him to join them.

"I can't believe what you're saying," utters Rosemary. "Please, go over it again so that we're clear as to precisely what happened."

They sit mesmerised as Henry relates his 'molestation' incident at the supermarket in detail, "Yes, it was all on account of my misplacing my brolly, which, by the way, they've kept as evidence."

"Your brolly?" asks Belinda.

"Yes. You see it happened thus: I was queueing at the store's check-out with my trolley of groceries, as of course were many others. There were two streams of shoppers waiting to pay; left and right channels. I was in the left one. When it eventually came to my turn I went to place my shopping on the conveyor belt as one does, I realised I had my brolly hooked over my right arm, so I went to hang it on the trolley handle as usual while I removed my shopping from the trolley, but I turned round a little too far and, perhaps because my peripheral vision is now rather poor, I inadvertently hung it on – this is terribly difficult – the lady's underwear in the adjacent channel, on what I now know to be a G-string, which was some inches above her jeans belt, slung low on her, er, broad hips. Her top, her tee-shirt, was riding so high that the lady had at least ten inches of exposed flesh, except for a large tattoo and her G-string. Naturally she took violent exception to this act and shouted out: 'Hey you! What the 'ell d'you think you're doing?' Or words to that effect." Henry takes a deep breath. "Then I reached for my brolly to correct this unfortunate misplacing of it, but in doing so I made matters worse. As I tugged, the crook of my brolly became fully hooked over her G-string. She swivelled round to remonstrate with me and then a shaven-headed, rough-looking man next to her, who I now know to be her husband, also grabbed my brolly. The three opposing forces all of a sudden tore her G-string in half! I staggered backwards and he's shouting 'bloody 'ell' and the lady yelled… excuse the language my good friends… 'shit, that bloody-well does it.'"

"Pretty voluble gal was she?" chortles Roger.

"She certainly was, she was also a very heavy lady. I guess something near twenty stone," adds Henry.

"Wearing a thwong? Wow!" exclaims Joe.

"Yes, indeed, as I said, a G-string, which was red in colour."

"Ye Gods!" utters Roger.

"The husband. He got aggressive, eh?"

"He wanted to, he raised his fists and shuffled about like a boxer in a ring, but I stood foursquare to him waving my brolly, shouting, 'how dare you threaten me!' He backed away, fortunately," smiles Henry.

"Wow! "What about the woman, what did she do?" starts Rosemary.

"She was leaping all over the place clutching her jeans, shouting that I was a pervert, I was molesting her, that I was a sex maniac. Just everybody was staring at us. It was awful." Henry sips his scotch.

"I say Henry, what was the tattoo?" asks Belinda. "Out of professional interest, of course."
"I only saw a part of it," says Henry.
"Yes, go on?" urges Joe.
"It was a dragon rampant in pink and blue with yellow fiery flames curled and looped in such a way as to, oh dear, as to point south." Henry makes a shape with his hands, and wriggles his fingers for the flames.
"You only saw part of it?"
"Waddya mean, point south?" says Roger, glass poised halfway to mouth.
"You know, downwards," says Henry pointing at the floor.
"Aaah! Her lower cleavage, eh?" leers Roger.
"Stop it, Roger," appeals Millicent.
"Gosh," says Joe.
"What happened next?" says Millicent, urging Henry on and noticing Stanley is sitting back with folded arms, looking at the ceiling.
"Suddenly I found myself being forced against the counter by the store's security lady, who told me not to move an inch. She pressed one arm against my throat while she pulled a mobile phone from her tunic with her free hand and yelled 'code-something-or-other' into it." Henry rolls his eyes.
"By jove, calling for back-up, eh? You must have looked a tough egg Henry!" chuckles Roger.
"I didn't know what to do." Henry looks around at the eager, expectant faces.
"Enough for a chap to develop a knicker fetish," adds

Henry's Brolly

Roger as he raises the bottle again. "Anyone?" Three nod their heads, he dispenses copious tots.

"What happened next, Henry?" asks Belinda.

"The police came dashing in ten minutes or so later. They bundled myself, the woman, a Mrs Lillian Hamper, her husband Frank and the security lady into an odds-and-sods room where they sat us down and took statements from each of us, then they arrested me and drove me to the police station. I was told if the CPS considered it appropriate, I would have to appear before the Plymington Magistrates' Court to answer these, er, awful charges. They didn't say exactly what." Henry spreads his arms.

"The CPS will almost certainly want you brought before a court. These days any apparent sexual attack will be pursued vigorously," says Belinda.

"I really can't understand any of this…" Henry starts to say, shaking his head.

"Easy, Henry old chap. Cheer up. Here," Roger empties the bottle into Henry's and his own glass.

"We'll support you, whatever," says Millicent.

"I ought to consult my solicitor. But–" Henry hesitates.

"Could be rather expensive, what?" says Rosemary.

Joe waves over the barman and orders another bottle of scotch, plus two gin and tonics.

"It isn't the expense," continues Henry, "but he's never inspired my confidence in last the few dealings I've had with him. Then again, it was only to do with wills and property."

"We do have an in-house legal advisor we can call upon," says Millicent.

"Sixpenny will, hic, have him firmly in her grasp, so ye can forget that," growls Roger.

"Nothing she'd like better than to see one of our group brought into disrepute and get us the boot."

"She could do that?" asks Joe gloomily, sipping his scotch.

"No. But the Board of Trustees could with her recommendation, if any of us are found to break the law in a manner so serious as to bring the establishment into disrespect," explains Belinda.

"Well then, consult and engage a top-lawyer from the city, hit 'em hard, old chap." says Roger.

"Would a high-flier take on such a case? Ex-MI5 man in charge of supermarket trolley, attacks dragon lady with bwolly." Joe draws an imaginary headline in the air with a hand. "With the pwospect of losing."

"Stop it Joe, it's not funny," berates Millicent.

"No m'dear. It's not. But that's what the headlines will shout should it become a nationwide case, especially if they get a whiff that Henry was MI5. Then you'll know what the word expensive means! Decency, weputation, wespect... all down the dear old Swanny." Joe sips his gin and tonic.

"You are out of order. Henry is a respectable, decent, honest man..." starts Millicent.

"Agreed. But if he's found to be a law-breaker, a sex pervert, we all, I mean we here, may well be tarred with the same brush. Tanner will rejoice and squash us flatter than an Olney pancake," says Rosemary.

"We must do something, something low-key, but what?" appeals Roger.

"We must be strong for Henry. We must stick together," appeals Millicent.

"Semantics," mutters Stanley, "won't help Henry one little bit."

"I know that two of my Rotary solicitor friends, although long retired, still retain connections with their legal firms in town. I could speak to them, perhaps get an introduction?" suggest Henry.

"I say," comes back Roger, "why not have Belinda here do the job for you?"

"Do the job, do the job? We're talking legal representation here, not fixing a leaky tap," says Rosemary.

"It's all right, we get the dwift… " starts Joe.

"Drift, drift? You and your darned ebbs and flows, Captain bloody Sea-Legs," says Roger.

"For goodness sake!" barks Rosemary. "Now, what about it, Belinda?"

"Yes, what about it, old girl. You were a heavy-weight in the Army Legal Service," recalls Joe.

"No win, no fee," chortles Roger.

"Don't be silly Joe, and less of the 'old girl' if you don't mind," retorts Belinda.

"Soweee."

"I was Military," says Belinda, "Totally different from civilian courts."

"Learning curve, what! Take a break from our bridge competitions," says Roger. "Expose yourself–"

"You're forever wanting to undress females, Roger Marshall, what is it with you?" snorts Rosemary.

"All in the mind love, you're quite safe, for now!"

Belinda emerges from a thought process, "Why don't you represent yourself, Henry? You could then be sure that your side of the incident, should it come to court, would be accurately portrayed?"

"I will give that serious consideration, Belinda, but if I go to court it will be a lamb to slaughter. I know little or nothing about legal procedures. My experience of courts has been to give evidence from behind closed doors, you, erm, understand?" says Henry.

"Undercover, eh?" says Joe, tapping the side of his nose with a forefinger, sipping someone elses gin and tonic. "You must have a story or two to tell, eh?"

"Well, perhaps I could help you… " admits Belinda. "Hey, that's my G and T you're supping Joe."

"Soweee."

"… although I haven't practiced for donkey's years, I must admit that I attend Plymington magistrate's Court and visit High Court in London, purely out of a professional interest. I do suggest, from my observations, that I could assist. I would be what they call 'a friend.'"

"What does that mean?" asks Millicent.

"It means I would be at Henry's side in court to advise him, but I wouldn't be allowed to address the court directly," says Belinda.

"Thank you, Belinda," acknowledges Henry. He ponders for a moment. "In that case, think I will stand for myself, if I am charged to appear, of course."

"Ye're both going in the right direction," grins Roger. "No stopping now."

"Hold fire," says Joe. "How can you be sure you can convince the magistwates of Henwy's innocence?"

"Oh, I can't be sure," admits Belinda. "A courtroom can be a place of hard knocks and nasty revelations."

"We'll give whatever support we can, won't we?" appeals Millicent, to all.

"That may not be easy," says Belinda. "My methods will ultimately depend on all of us playing a part."

"Methods? Ultimately? We? All?" barks Rosemary, askance.

"Yes we all. I'm thinking of a way forward as to how we may confront, defeat, these outrageous accusations," says Belinda, "as a team."

"To a successful conclusion," toasts Roger.

"To success," agrees Millicent, delicately lifting her glass.

"To shucksess," intones Joe, draining his gin and tonic.

"Roger, your toupee is, er, somewhat askew," grins Rosemary, leaning back, more relaxed.

"What, what are ye sayin'? My–"

"Your wig," Joe places his hands on his head and shimmies them about.

Roger adjusts his headpiece, "Kay now?"

"Sort of. But the ginger doesn't match your grey side-locks–"

"Shut up, Joe."

"Go along with that," gurgles Rosemary, sipping her drink. "Not the best match I've seen."

They start to chatter idly to each other. Henry leans over, speaks into Roger's ear. "Was Belinda a good a lawyer, Roger?"

"First-class. Successful career in the Army Legal

Service and afterwards in civvy-street at Lincoln's Inn, she's always popping up there for dinner with her old pals. She has a reputation for being unconventional in her presentation, nevertheless she was a winner by all accounts. I saw her in action myself a few years ago," adds Roger. "Magnificent! Fine stance, fine approach, fine body, great tits, legs like Marilyn–"

"Roger… please!" protests an overhearing Millicent.

"She'll do you proud, Henry old bean. With her by your side you shouldn't be the least bit worried."

Belinda speaks up, "Should it come to pass, we must prepare carefully and choreograph our presentation to present Henry's case in such a way as to leave no doubt in the magistrates' minds that he acted in all innocence; that he's such a gentleman he is incapable of attacking anyone, let alone launching a sexual attack on a young woman in a crowded supermarket. Then, crucially, there's Henry's failing eyesight to take into consideration. This would seem to have played an important part in these unfortunate proceedings."

"You keep saying 'we', Belinda," poses Millicent. "You seem to be embracing us in your plans to prove our Henry innocent."

"Embrace? Hmm. Unfortunate choice of word under the circumstances. But yes of course, we shall all need to be involved in presenting Henry's case," says Belinda, waving her cane like a baton.

"How…?" starts Rosemary.

"First I must speak to Plymington Magistrate's Clerk of Court to advise that should the CPS decide to prosecute, Henry will represent himself, and that I will

Henry's Brolly

act as his so-called 'friend' in court. That agreed, we shall then secure and review CPS's evidence. That will include victim and witness statements, also there is bound to be CCTV footage from the store of the, er, incident. This will be all-revealing," says Belinda.

"Ah, ha! So we'll get to see this almighty tug-o-war between our Henry's brolly and this dragon-lady's sexy thong on film, eh?" cackles Roger.

"Roger. That is inappropriate language. Do contain yourself. Please?" growls Rosemary.

"Reprimand accepted Ma'am. I shall remain self-contained," Roger says with a broad grin on his face.

"Good."

"Hey, this won't interfere with our bridge competition will it? We've got the townees on the run!"

"Could do. I can't say when or how long Henry's case would go on for. If it ever comes to court that is."

"I've got a lecture date at Sandhurst next month," adds Roger. "Bomb disposal in the forties and fifties."

"And in a fortnights time, I am to be a marshal at the Plymington Yacht Club's annual wegatta. I really ought not to miss that," says Joe. "We have international competition, fwom New Zealnd."

Belinda, noncommittal, shrugs. "I simply don't know. We should be prepared; the sooner the better."

"Righto, Belinda, tell us about this plan of action of yours," asks Henry, sitting back, more at ease.

"Under the circumstances we must assume that charges will be brought, and court papers issued as to when Henry will be obliged to appear before the magistrates," she explains.

"So what do we do meanwhile?" asks Millicent.

"We must prepare. We need measured, military thinking. First we should drum up support for Henry. We shall petition all of Wardley's residents and record positive character references for him. Rosemary, you are the Chair of the Resident's Committee." Belinda looks at Rosemary. "I ask you to take that on board?"

"Consider it done," Rosemary agrees, nodding.

"I'm looking for a minimum of seventy-percent to sign, agreeing that Henry is of excellent character, has caused no ill-will or mischief within these hallowed walls, etc., etc. Yes?" Belinda demands.

"Yes. Goddit! I'll round up ninety percent in favour – or else," boasts Rosemary.

"Let's get Tanner's signature at the top of the list. Heh, heh!" chuckles Joe. "That'd be a bonus."

"Good luck with that," says Millicent.

"Sixpenny? Sign a character reference for one of us, for Henry? No chance," says Roger.

"Then we'll bloody-well forge it," says Rosemary.

"Her signature as our Superintendent would be beneficial," adds Belinda. "Excellent suggestion, Roger."

"We'll pummel the lady into submission behind the bike shed," grins Joe.

"There is also Dudley Fortescue Senior, our esteemed Chairman of the Board of Trustees."

Stanley rises to his feet: "I'm feeling tired, please excuse me," he walks out of the room.

They watch him leave. Roger frowns, "Doesn't seem too keen on helping Henry, does he?"

"Curious that the man quits our company at the oddest of moments."

"Secondly," says Belinda, looking round, "we shall need a shopping trolley."

"A what?" utters Roger, eyes widening.

"A shopping twolley? What for?" demands Joe.

"We need a supermarket trolley," continues Belinda, "the same sort as the one used by Henry at the store where he was arrested. But I guess they're all pretty much the same."

"How do we get–" starts Millicent.

"Initiative people. Military initiative. I am looking for a man with such initiative, Joe?"

"I'll round up Walter Masters and see what he can do," assents Joe, quick on the uptake.

"Now, for our rehearsals, which we shall need to undertake several times to enhance our chances–"

"Would the lady flesh that out some?" chuckles Roger.

"Again, a poor choice of word!" says a haughty Rosemary.

"All for it m'dear! Do continue. Belinda," says Roger.

"The man's sex mad," jeers Rosemary.

"Yeah, yeah." intones Roger. "Ye should spend time at the Crown and Sceptre m'dear. Disco's great, it's therapeutic and uplifting. Place is full of bounce on Saturday evenings, ye know what I mean. D'ye want to come with me to my favourite watering-hole?"

"Is this man altogether with it?" cries Rosemary. "Really. A night club. Brrrrrr!"

Belinda continues, ignoring the exchange, "We shall

need to demonstrate to the magistrates what did actually happen at that supermarket. So I will draw up a list of the parts each of us will play–"

"PARTS!"

"PLAY!"

Crash! Bang! The common room door collides against the wall as it is thrown violently open. Stalking through the doorway is one angry Moira Sixpenny. She stops, turns her head, eyes alight on the breakfast crew seated together. She strides over to them, eyes exuding pure hatred, bellowing, "I most certainly will not vouch for Henry Osbourne!"

Other residents seated around the common room fall silent, keenly watching and listening to the very irate Superintendent.

"Oh, ho!" barks Roger. "What shall ye make of this interloper, dear friends?"

"You and your stupid, crude remarks Roger Marshall," yells Moira Sixpenny. "I've never been so, so, so insulted by a pack of, of, of... old, old, people such as the likes of, of–"

"Geriatrics is the word you seek, m'dear. And from one such, may I suggest you calm down."

Stanley idles in the doorway, head at an angle, as if to hear better what is being said.

"Calm down, calm down," storms Sixpenny. "I will not calm down. I have had enough."

"For the life of me, why are you being so bloody aggressive?" demands Rosemary. "We are merely–"

"You listen to me, Rosemary Carter-Smythe, I've had it up to here with you and your so-called friends conspiring to get me removed from my position here," shouts Sixpenny.

"Far from it," interrupts Joe, "we want you to be pweserved, indefinitely."

"In aspic–" says Roger, behind his a hand.

"Shut up, Roger. Superintendent Sixpenny, why would we entertain such a thing?" asks Rosemary.

"You are wital in the great scheme of things," adds Joe.

"Whoever put a silly idea like wanting you to leave us into your head ?" says Roger.

"Aah, you're here to tell us residents are complaining about their breakfast being on the coolish side."

"We shall defend ourselves to the hilt."

"Wasn't an underdone sausage was it?" says Roger.

"It is due to the lack of toast, I'm sure," says Belinda, grinning.

Sixpenny looks at them incredulously. "You are all utterly barking mad," she spins on her heel. With a parting shot, "I will report this episode to Colonel Fortescue of the Board of Trustees. Then we shall see what you make of that!" she storms past Stanley, still hovering in the doorway.

"Now look what you've done," says Belinda, rising from her armchair with the aid of her cane.

"What," says Roger, tweaking his ear device, "have we done?"

"Pissed orf the untouchable Tanner," says Rosemary, imitating him.

"She is such an inelegant lady," observes Millicent, also standing up.

"Definitely wude," adds Joe, lifting, peering, shaking an empty bottle.

"The lady doth disapprove of us," smirks Roger.

"Whatever gave you that idea?" says Joe.

* * *

Early evening at six-thirty, the breakfast crew gather in the quiet lounge; most of the residents having wandered off to prepare for dinner. Belinda, leaning on her cane, stands before them and explains her plan, "I want to present to the magistrates the events as they unfolded at the supermarket, to prove that Henry was merely being absent-minded where he hung his brolly, that he didn't deliberately lodge it on the lady's G-string. So it'll be best if we rehearse that scene so that we can portray to the court exactly what happened."

"I asked Walter to bwing his tea cart as a substitute for a supermarket trolley," says Joe, "Hopefully, minus dirty cwockery."

"We'll depict those who were involved in this drama, Henry's confrontation, as best we can. We will be under close scrutiny in court. Not a word to be spoken, except Henry's narration, so that the magistrates will get the full import of what happened. Also, we shall be better informed if and when I obtain copies of the supermarket video tapes from CPS. Henry was astute enough to remember each person's character and appearance." Belinda picks up a clip-board. "So we have five players: Henry himself, the 'victim', the large lady, one Lillian Hamper, who says Henry sexually molested her. Now then..." Belinda absently rattles her pen between her teeth, "... who amongst us would best fit that bill; it ought to be a largish female–"

All eyes swivel, focusing on Rosemary.

"Me?" she retorts. "Don't be bloody ridiculous! I'm certainly not of such proportions as described."

"You're just perfect for the part m'dear," chuckles Roger. "Imagine you sporting a thong. Wow!"

"Then there's the belligerent husband, Frank Hamper," continues Belinda, ignoring this side-play, "Well, I think you will be good in that part, Roger. You'll have to learn Hamper's Cockney idiom though."

"Me, belligerent? Load of old tosh. And what d'ye mean, learn Cockney idiom?"

"Your English is mangled and frequently mixed with Scottish expletives."

"I do not mangle," retorts Roger. "And I do not explete."

"Well, the Scottish part of your vocabulary fwequently does both," observes Joe.

An irritated Roger throws up his arms, "ye Sassenachs are all the bloody same. And you Joe, I'm werry, werry weary wove wones English."

"Little Miss Muffet, to you," snarls Joe.

"Wha… "

"Cockney vernacular," explains Belinda. "Stuff it!"

"Yes, cut the crap m'dears," says Rosemary, "I'll do Lillian Hamper, okay?"

"Hey-up, Belinda, you said we would be miming–" cries Roger.

"Just testing, Roger, just testing," smiles Belinda, as she ticks off two names on her clip-board.

"I say, that's a bit rich. Just testing?"

A smiling, Belinda says, "Next the security lady; seemingly we'll need a fair-minded person. Millicent. You fit her type perfectly."

"Me, a security guard? Oh dear," purrs Millicent, fluttering her eyelashes innocently.

"Yes," says Belinda, "you will get to learn what it takes to be a security person guarding a supermarket."

"Oh dear," repeats Millicent. Not adverse to the idea, on second thoughts.

"Then we have the man tending Henry's till. An important witness who should be impartial. Looking at our now depleted cast list, we must ask Joe, who's impartiality is known to all, to play his part."

Joe nods his assent, "Agweed."

"Henry, does that seem to be all the parties involved?" asks Belinda, putting down her clip-board..

"Yes. Except for the police. But they came later when we were moved into a side room," says Henry.

"Right, folks. Today will be a talk through. We shall work up to a dress rehearsal as the evidence and the date of Henry's case is given to us."

Roger says, looking at his watch and sniffs, "Dinner. We eat first?"

"Yes," agrees Belinda, "then we return here at eight-thirty."

"No Corry Street for you tonight, Rosemary. Real thing instead, what?"

Henry's Brolly

Rosemary sniffs: "I do not watch soaps. Now, I think I'll tinkle the ivories for a few minutes just to relax," she rises, walks over to the home's old Steinway grand, seats herself on the padded stool, raises her hands, a comfortable flexing of the fingers, poised…

"I say," starts Roger, "bit of an overlap, what d'ye say, Joe?"

"Hmmm–" Joe pauses for effect.

"Shut up you two," admonishes Belinda. "Rosemary's stature is not up for discussion. Understood?'

They, smile, stand up, dinner momentarily on hold, and wend their way around armchairs to sit and listen to their favourite ex-concert pianist. The lady rises to the occasion, hammering the keys with a rousing rendition of a Gilbert & Sullivan's piece.

The crew join in with humorous word-descriptions of their adversaries, and clap along.

* * *

"Wosemary, your performance last evening as Mrs Hamper was qwite amusing, it was that slinky walk between the armchairs we had awanged to wepresent the supermarket's till area. We weceived so much laughter from the other wesidents," he tongs two rashers of bacon on a wavering plate. He looks up, an old chum nods at the sausages, he obliges. Two juicy farm sausages land on the man's plate.

"No, it was Roger, Joe, that inspired most laughter. Your cheering him on as he grabbed Henry's brolly and tried to hook Rosemary's pretend G-string."

"Most undignified," mutters Rosemary. "He almost succeeded."

"As were you, chasing him out of the room."

"I am far too busy to listen to this." Rosemary retorts, placing slices of bread on the toaster's moving rack.

"Anyway, I think our group's rehearsals in preparation for Henwy's appearance in court are proving to be so good that we ought to undertake the home's Christmas Panto this year," says Joe.

"Get focussed Joe. Look, old Mrs James wants some baked beans, ladle some out for me, I'm too busy with the toaster."

"Yes, we do need another volunteer. He was a real creep, but I admit Stanley was good at the toaster."

"And I'm not?" Rosemary retorts.

"Well..."

"Joe's got a point. All this drama business. You'd be admirable as Widow Twanky." says Roger, ladling out tinned peaches, kumquats, cherries and fresh grapes into a large bowl and placing it onto a shaking tray. "It's that fine bod of yours–"

"Scrub that. Anyhow, Widow Twanky is always played by a fellah. You'd be just right for the part," says Rosemary.

"Who says we're going to have Aladdin this year?" interrupts Millicent.

"It's proposed by the Residents Entertainment Committee's Chairman. Nothing firmed up. Yet."

"I'm fed up with the rehearsals, setting up the lounge as if a courtroom, pwancing around to the other residents' amusement. Surely we're weady for the weal thing," pleads Joe.

"Any news?" asks Rosemary, looking around at the squad. "About Henry's case?"

"It's about time we heard," adds Roger.

"Henry's at reception checking the mail, as he has done for the past three weeks," says Millicent, as she stirs the sloshy pile of scrambled egg to keep it hot through-and-through.

"Darned-well the sooner the better. I'm alright portraying that Hamper fellah, but Belinda is hinting that I get my arms tattooed for dramatic effect. She can forget that."

"She's simply taking the rise out of you Roger, as with the Cockney accent. Anyway, it would only be artists make-up."

"What about you, having a dragon painted on your ar–"

"Watch it!"

"Er, lower back."

"He's back," exclaims Millicent, dropping her scoop with a clatter.

"Back, who is back?" exclaims Roger.

"Henry. Oh, he does look rather agitated."

They all stop their preparing and serving and look up. Henry walks into the buffet area with Belinda. He waves a letter. "I have a court date," he says grimly.

* * *

Geriatricks 1

"After four weeks of dramatic re-enactments, are we fully prepared?" enquires Belinda as the breakfast squad gather in the home's reception area at eight-thirty. The men in military-style parkas, ladies dolled up in fur-collared overcoats and scarves to combat a frosty, chilly morning. She raises an eyebrow at Roger's choice of a multi-coloured head gear with a bobble and his dark unshaven face, and Joe in tweeds.

"Rosemary," sniffs Roger, "You smell like the perfume counter at John Lewis. Delightful."

"I decided that Lilly Hamper would be the sort to use lots of smell," she replies.

Their re-enactment clothes, bundled in plastic bags, are heaped in a supermarket trolley stood near to the entrance door. Belinda walks over, tapping the trolley's handle with her walking stick to draw attention. Then... she frowns, sniffing: "My God, what is that awful stench, and where...?" her quivering nose leads her to bend, sniff in, around the trolley basket. She locates one particular bundle as being the offender. "And who does this belong to?" she demands, pointing.

"Ah ha," says Roger, "must be that old pair of trousers I asked Walter to find for me. I need to wear something to look like Frank Hamper on the CCTV. Walter says he got it from a wooden chest he stores old clothes in, left by, er, departing residents, destined for the charity shops, he says."

Belinda draws apart the plastic bag. "Oh, this is too much," she stands back, aghast at the awful pong.

Joe peers at the half-opened bag, "I think those belonged to old Tobias, I can tell by–"

Henry's Brolly

"He died more than a year ago, so how is it that his trousers are still... oh, never mind," says Belinda.

"Smells like twenty dead wats," says Joe, sniffing. "It'll make the justices sit up and take notice, by heck!"

"Attention," barks Belinda, moving further away. "Have we got all of our appropriate clothing and gear for our reenactment in court? Henry, your brolly, let me see it, it is important."

"My spare one, yes, I have it here," he lifts and twirls it for emphasis. "And my best suit for my court room apearance, is in here." He lift a small black suitcase.

Mute nods from the others, then from Millicent, "Belinda, repeat the times again if you would."

"The minibus will arrive shortly at ten o'clock, then we move off in good order. We are due at Plymington Court at ten-thirty. Our case, Henry's, is scheduled to be heard at approximately eleven-thirty. I've allowed plenty of time for us to find somewhere to change into our demonstration clothing," says Belinda.

"Damned cold outside!" explodes Roger, rubbing his hands.

"And where's the she-ogre to see us orf?" adds Joe.

"That's enough," barks Belinda.

"Kept her head below the parapet since you collected a ninety-five percent sign-up concerning Henry's character. And all credit to Colonel Fortescue for adding his siggy as well. She must be really pissed–"

"Hush yourself. We're in the spotlight here," Belinda inclines her head towards receptionist Irene.

Roger, in a mock whisper, "Bet Tanner's being comforted, embraced, by that Stanley fellah someplace."

"Well, he was rather miffed at not having been invited to participate in our charade," adds Rosemary.

"Rosemary. You got all the right togs with you?" queries Roger, changing tack with a broad grin.

"What on Earth do you mean, the right togs?" asks Rosemary.

"Y'know, G-string, tight jeans, tight short top ... all that," he leers.

"Oh, you are awful," retorts Rosemary.

"My right as your hubby, m'dear, to know if you're wearing sexy underwear. Especially in a court of law."

"Hubby?" frowns Rosemary.

"You're playing Lilly Hamper, I'm playing hubby Frank."

"The neanderthal is showing in you, Roger, don't get too carried away."

Belinda limps in-between the two 'Hampers'. "Will you two stop bickering and save your energy for the courtroom," she cranes her neck to peer. "Ah, ha, here's the minibus."

The team crowd around the doorway with their bundles as the driver draws up, opens his door, steps down and walks into reception to assist them. Belinda shows him the trolley. He raises an eyebrow, sniffing but says nothing as he trundles the trolley outside to the rear of the minibus, twists the handle, swings up the rear door and, with Roger and Joe's help, hefts the trolley and bundles inside. The others, and Henry with his suitcase, climb chattering, into the minibus and snuggle down to keep warm.

"All aboard?" the driver yells as he squirms his way into his seat and straps himself in.

"All accounted for," agrees Belinda, tapping his shoulder. "Drive off when ready. Heater full on please."

The minibus moves out of Wardley's grounds to join the traffic stream heading for the town centre.

* * *

Belinda consults her watch as they travel into town. "Are you quite ready for this, Henry?" she queries.

"Yes, I'm fine, I've learned my opening argument almost by heart and I have also, with the aid of some of my old colleagues, conducted extensive research into criminal court procedures. But I have a question, can you be sure the magistrates will allow us to undertake our re-enactment of what actually happened?"

"No. But I did have a quiet word with the clerk last week, a friend of an old school chum. I argued the point that we are allowed to use reasonable support material in court. The extent of that remains a matter of debate, so, when we appear in the courtroom with a supermarket trolly and a bunch of doppelgangers, the bench may well challenge the use of such 'material'. So Henry, I suggest, if that comes to pass, that we stand our ground and firmly argue that the CCTV footage, to be presented by the CPS solicitor, is quite inadequate to properly demonstrate what actually happened," says Belinda.

"This sounds very complicated, Belinda," says Henry. "But I do appreciate what you are doing for me."

"Well, everybody, except the magistrates themselves of course, have been warned as to what I plan to do, with no dissension to date. Let me add that I am confident all will be well."

They approach Plymington Magistrate's Court and the driver swings round to access the rear of the building. The squad dismount, the driver helping them unload their trolly and bags. They shuffle and shiver, subdued, before an impassive policeman in winter uniform, stood at ease before a steel door. Belinda spies a doorbell located to one side of it. She inclines her head at the copper. He nods, she presses the button. After a minute another uniformed policeman opens the door, does a double-take at the number before him and queries their presence. Belinda explains the who, the why and the whatever!

The officer runs down the list of names on his clipboard, then smartly splits them into three groups. The prisoner, his 'friend' Belinda and the public. "Now, the public, that's you four, you go to the posh entrance round at the front. Inside you will find an usher roaming about in the main concourse. He will guide you to your court room… " he looks down, "… number four. Right, off you go!" The four lift their bags out of the trolly, tuck them under their arms and head to the front entrance. "Where we shall find a coffee, cake and scone-room, I bloody-well hope," mutters Roger.

"And a, loo too" sing-songs Joe.

"You two stay put," orders the policeman to Henry and Belinda. "And – what is that?" he asks, pointing to the supermarket trolley.

"It is our defence property" advises Henry.

"Your what?" he policeman queries.

"D-e-f-e-n-c-e -p-r-o-p-e-r-t-y," Henry spells it out.

"Watch your lip, matey," threatens the officer.

"I do apologise for my friend, officer. He is under some pressure," gushes Belinda. "But the trolley is to play a vital part in the court proceedings. Without it we won't be able to put over our case properly."

"The suitcase and brolly?" The officer points to the two objects sat in the trolley's basket.

"The brolly is part of our presentation, it is essential to our renactment scene," Belinda adds. "The suitcase contains Henry's best suit, for his appreance. He wants to look his best."

The officer grabs Henry's brolly, examines it, fingering the spike. "I'll have to clear this, could be used as a weapon. Stay here," he steps back inside the door and reaches for a wall-mounted phone, punches a button and then speaks in a low voice while glancing at them from time to time. He nods, beckons them. "Right, in you both come, suitcase, brolly and trolley," he tags the three items and wheels the trolley to one side before leading the two of them into a corridor of doors to show them into an empty room. "In here," he says, with a sweep of his arm. He holds up and rattles a bunch of keys ominously as they pass inside. "No monkey business mind, or you'll get locked up proper, goddit?"

They both nod and sit on a bench. The officer says, "When my phone rings, it means the Clerk of the Court is calling for me to move your valuable presence into the court room."

"Yes, I understand," says Henry.

"No you don't. It means my pal, and he's a big chap,

will escort prisoner into court room number four, where he will be properly addressed by the Clerk, CPS and the Beaks. And you… " he addresses Belinda, "… will now proceed to the main concourse where the usher will tell you where you can sit in the court room." Henry sits, forlorn in the cell-like room as Belinda gives him a tiny wave, and with the aid of her cane, limps after the officer via an internal route to the main concourse.

* * *

"I've got a craving for a tot of Bells," crows Roger, as the Wardley four wait patiently, queuing at the scanning post inside the main entrance. Belinda materialises, nods and leans patiently on her cane as they get ready to move one-by-one between the scanning bridge.

"Do we get fwisked?" asks Joe, holding his arms akimbo.

"I should jolly-well hope so," chuckles Rosemary, "after going to all this trouble." She flaunts herself in a mincing stage-strut to rhythmic clapping from the squad as she passes through the scanner bridge.

The others follow, under the stern gaze of the operator, a lady. A male assistant, stood to one side, is busy checking each parcel of clothing. "What are these for?" And then, "what is that awful smell?" He waves a hand in front of his face. "Phew. Jeesus! I need air. It's this one," he points an accusing finger.

"Defwumigate it," suggests Joe. "Else ye pong will linger longer," a grin from the squad at this Joeism.

"I asked," says the assistant, wrinkling his nose, eyes

streaming, almost overcome by the sour odour from old Tobias' trousers, "what are dees items of clothing for?"

"Dey are part of our case," mocks Joe.

"Evidence!" Roger says pompously.

The operative lady gives the two men a strange look, confers with her assistant and, after a brief talk, waves over a tall, black-cloaked, usher. The man swirls up to the group. More discussion. He says he will let them pass, but he will be confer with the Clerk of Court before they are permitted to take their bundles of clothing into the court itself. "Wait here–"

The team stand with Belinda, clutching their bags. "Where is the trolley?" asks Millicent.

"And the brolly," adds Rosemary.

"All is well," says Belinda, "They are placed in a cloakroom nearby, under armed guard.

"Ye jest, surely," grins Roger. Belinda smiles.

The cloaked usher sweeps over. Yes, they may carry their parcels into court, after a further check at the door. Their case is to be heard at eleven-thirty, as near as can be predicted.

The cheered-up group stroll between suits, smart business outfits and the hoi poi-loi, towards the rows of occupied seats situated along the centre of the concourse, adjacent to court room four.

"Bit of a jamboree, eh? Busier here than the old Dubai souk, what?" utters Roger, looking around for somewhere to sit down.

"Not a patch on the Hong Kong market," joins Joe, also looking about.

"Ah, ha, do I espy our Moira Sixpenny and Stanley hovering yonder in the crowd?" says Roger.

"And, believe it or not, next to them is Colonel Dudley Fortescue," observes Rosemary.

"Come to cheer us on," says Joe.

"Or see us get our cwomeuppance," groans Joe.

"I spy ye old coffee shop over there. Onward, good folk," Roger waves for them to follow. He elbows his way into the crowded bistro where several groups of solicitors, clients, officials, police officers in immaculate white shirts, smart trousers, black-belts adorned with handcuffs, radios and kit, and suits clutching bundles of files, holding mobiles to their ear; others earnestly chatting to one another, sipping coffees.

The breakfast four again find themselves with nowhere to sit to wait out time before their court case.

"Back outside," grunts Rosemary. "Like a bloody black hole in here."

"Hold hard. Woger, pass me the plastic bag with Tobias' trousers in it," Joe asks. Roger does so. Joe unties the knot, spreads the bag's mouth, exposing the ragged, brown pair of tweed trousers. Head held to one side, he saunters behind a group of five solicitor-types seated around a chrome coffee table. He bends down, casually drops the bag under the chair of a short, tubby man, pressing a legal point on his colleagues. Joe returns to the group. "I give them three, four minutes," he says, mouthing his words for the benefit of Roger.

They look on, observe sniffs, handkerchiefs being tugged out, noses wiped, surreptitious looks at each other. First of all, one shoves his files into a briefcase, another folds his laptop, a third glares at the hapless man who stands up, wrinkles his nose, motions the fifth, a lady, to join him outside. They all move off and the squad quickly move in. They sit down, Roger secures the offending bag then heads over toward the bar to buy much-needed refreshment.

Belinda raises her voice over the background chatter to address them: "Now, when we get in, no nonsense, this is a serious place and mobile phones will be turned off. Millicent, I trust we will not hear the 633 Squadron bearing down upon us during court proceedings?"

Millicent smiles, shaking her head.

"I say, Rosemary," barks Roger, coming up with a tray of coffees and croissants, and eyeing Rosemary's corpulent backside, overlapping her seat, "ye don't happen to have fiery dragon tattooed on your ba, ba, ba, backside–"

Rosemary half turns, she lifts a lip, snarling. "Do take off that daft tea-cosy when you address a lady."

"The tattoo is not relevant," interrupts Belinda. "Besides, it would draw the magistrates' attention away from Henry hooking the brolly onto, er, Lilly Hamper's G-string. Now be quiet, Roger."

"Bless me da'hling, ye're taking all the fun out of it, what?"

Three mouths open to respond, but are halted pre-sentence; a smart blonde lady wearing a fawn jacket and trouser suit and sporting a white security badge, walks up to them. "Belinda Huxley?" she asks. Belinda rises, shakes the proffered hand, breathing in a waft Cologne Bigarade exuding from the lady.

"I am the prosecuting CPS lawyer on Mr Osbourne's case: Miz Stella Bullett," she announces.

Roger chortles along with Joe, mouthing 'bullett' with raised eyebrows at each other, "quick on the draw, I bet?" The two admire the shapely legs and the Jane Shilton boots. "No spurs," whispers Joe.

Miz Bullett ignores the repartees. "I just popped out to see if I could find you. Fortunately I had the help of a very observant usher; t'was he who sent me in your direction."

"What can I do for you, Miz Bullett?" Belinda asks politely.

"My approaching you like this is somewhat outside the norm but I want to clarify one or two points. You, being of the military legal profession, are Henry Osbourne's representative in court today I believe?"

"No I'm not. I am long retired, I do not practice, I'm merely here to advise Mr Osbourne as a 'friend.'"

"Gratis?" Miz Bullett asks.

"Of course Miz Bullett. Henry is a very good friend. We live together in a community where we fend, tend and support each other, where and when necessary." Belinda frowns. Where is all this leading?

"More fool you." Stella Bullett casts a heavy eye over Millicent, Roger and Joe. "It is common knowledge that some residents of Wardley Officers' Residential Home have a certain reputation in the town."

"Really?" Belinda raises innocent eyebrows.

"Pompous, wealthy, stand-offish, do-nothing-for-the-community, bunch of cantankerous oldies."

"That is outrageous, and quite untrue."

"This your first taste of a criminal court, Belinda?"

"No. But I'll probably find it lacks the pomp and ceremony of a military courts martial."

"Oh, I don't know. We have our moments. Er, may we speak discreetly if you please?" the two edge a away from the others. "You and Mr Osbourne requested of the court that you be permitted to carry out a demonstration of some sort, so as to present his case more fully?"

"Yes, we understand we can present reasonable support material, and that this will focus the attention of the magistrates, and indeed yourselves at CPS, on the way this incident unravelled to the detriment of all concerned, in particular Henry Osbourne, who is an upright, honest, honourable man. Also to show that this case ought not to have been prosecuted at all," states Belinda.

"Oh, I've seen them come and go, these elderly, perverted, so-called upright, honest, honourable men. It would be best for him if he pleaded guilty." Miz Bullett angles her head, giving a thin smile.

"Surely we can't discuss this out here?"

"Under my questioning, I expect Mr Osbourne to fold and admit guilt," boasts the CPS lady.

"It sounds to me as if your mind isn't as open as it should be," retorts Belinda with concern.

"I am a prosecutor. I simply want you to understand that the court won't tolerate any undue theatricals which would lead to a possible miscarriage of justice."

"Really, Miz Bullett, do not presume we would want to cloud the issue in any way."

"I am a little puzzled as to why a gentleman of his

stature should want to represent himself. I wouldn't have thought it was a matter of money?" she shakes her head to hear all the better over the noisy chatter.

"I couldn't say," replies Belinda dryly. "Anyway, Mr Osbourne has researched the situation thoroughly and has amassed significant procedural information to be able to adequately represent himself."

"Egg-head sort, is he?"

"Some might say."

"Look, lady," Miz Bullett hesitates, "I would hate your so-called comeback to end in disaster."

"This is no comeback," Belinda smiles. "I am retired… " now with edge, "… but I remain a member of Lincoln's Inn."

"Oh!" says Miz Bullett, taken aback.

Touché. Belinda smiles to herself.

Stella Bullet frowns, looking at her wristwatch, "I must take my leave. I have a case before Mr Osbourne is called forward," she swirls round, departs, heels click-clacking on the stone floor.

"Trouble, Belinda?" asks Millicent.

"No, my dear, no trouble, just sniffy about us," she says as she sits down. "I want you to remember, on no account must you utter a word in court, paticularly while we are enacting Henry's assault scene."

"I say, that's not on," interjects Roger. "No hurrahs, ya-boos or dragon-lady roars?"

"Absolutely no ribald jokes or obscenities. You are an officer and a gentleman. Mmmm?" says Belinda.

Roger salutes the lady, "Yes ma'am, no ma'am, three bags–"

"And you, Joe, keep that packet of chocolate digestives out of sight, this isn't a picnic on the Yacht Club's veranda flirting with the admiral's girlfriend," instructs Belinda.

"If only!"

"Now then, I remind you all… " ignoring Roger and Joe's levity, " … we mime the whole scene, except Henry, who will give a commentary of what happened when he rises for the last word, and destroys the CPS, Miz Bullett's, so-called evidence against him."

"The shopping trolley?" interrupts Joe.

"It will be brought into court at same time as Henry, is" replies Belinda.

"Where's the brolly?" queries Roger.

"The one we used at rehearsals is with the trolley. The original brolley, wielded in the fracas, is with CPS, who will no doubt demonstrate to Henry's disadvantage, how it was manipulated to 'undress' Lilly Hamper in public."

"We take our cue from Henry's narrative?" asks Millicent.

"Precisely. Also remember, your actions must be in relatively slow-motion."

"Wike this?" Joe Baker slips off his seat to create a dyingswan movement in slow-motion, rising on one leg and waving an arm. They all laugh.

"No, Joe. We must not to make the court laugh, or even chuckle or even smile. We are here to persuade the bench that Henry was merely somewhat clumsy in where he hung his brolly, and that it was nothing more than that. Remember, this is the sole purpose of the exercise. Any levity will be seen as mocking the court and they won't stand for it. They may even dismiss this as a pantomime if it's seen to be poking fun at Henry's so-called victim, or the CPS solicitor for that matter. And don't even think about locking eyes with the magistrates," she looks hard at Roger, "especially if any of the magistrates are women."

"They will not get to admire my handsome countenance if we cannot go eye-to-eye," grins Roger,

"Balderdash is all you speak these days, Roger. Now, any questions?" Belinda looks round. "None, okay."

"Twenty minutes everybody," observes Joe, eyeing the wall clock. "So prepare thyselves, slaves, let us not turneth this into a comedy of errors."

Rosemary rolls her eyes, "This is not a bloody theatre, Joe."

"Could've fooled me," Roger replies, looking pointedly around at the ongoing activity in the café.

They move into the concourse, stand outside court room four's entrance to wait and to ponder. After a few minutes the cloaked usher comes up to them, "Case number two: Crown verses Osbourne? You may move into the courtroom if you please, ladies and gentlemen."

"Who is on the bench this morning my good man?" asks Roger of the usher, who holds the court room door open for the squad to pass through.

The man blinks, smiles, common ground established, "The chairman is a Sir Thomas Crombie, sitting with Mr Geoffrey Makepiece and Mrs Susan Peters."

"Good uns, eh? You can tell me," winks Roger.

"Sir Thomas Crombie is pompous and, er, something of an–"

"Ass?" finishes Roger.

"I wouldn't go that far, sir. Mr Makepiece is an old fossil who needs lots of prompting, clarification of argument and wants to hear everything twice. Mrs Peters is a stick-in-the-mud Town Councillor which may have something to do with her being a local archaeologist. She will reach for the magistrates' guide book every time." The usher eyes the open door, hinting that Roger pass through.

"Know the Star and Garter, Fawley Road, my good man?" beams Roger, standing his gound.

"Yeees ... umm?"

"Meet me there tonight, an hour after sunset. I'll buy you a pint, or two."

The usher smiles and says, "Crombie tends to go for leniency. Makepiece uses a ouija board to aid his decision making and he is rarely wrong. Susan Peters is a long-standing member of the local magic circle, she has a passion for tarot cards and she is said to convey an ethereal aura at times. Oh yes, get your people to lay their bundles in the alcove next to the public seating area on the right, you will see it."

"Thanks, Mr... " Roger peers closely at the usher's security badge, "Tits Welts?"

"It's Titus sir, Titus Wells. And I'm non-alcoholic!" The usher waves Roger into the court room.

"On the wagon, eh? Chin-up, won't last! Pity about the Star and Garter," Roger pokes the man in the ribs, laughs, hurries through the door to catch up with the others.

The usher slowly raises a second finger at Roger's disappearing figure.

Roger retorts, not looking round, "You should get that finger bandaged, Tits … before it goes septic!"

* * *

In the court room the breakfast squad, after placing their bundles of clothes in the alcove as directed, push open a side gate to grope past several already-seated peoples' knees and feet, to seat themselves in the row of fold-down seats in the rapidly filling courtroom. Belinda heads for a row of benches in the centre of the court room, reserved for lawyers. She places her folders on the bench beside her, leaning on her cane.

"Ye Gods," exclaims Roger, "Heaving in here, just like the 4-Sure betting shop on a Saturday morning."

"You would know, wouldn't you?" says Rosemary, bullying and shuffling to fit into her narrow space.

"That's better," smirks Roger, "knee-to-knee at last darlin'. A dream come true." He pats Rosemary's knee.

Rosemary siezes and squeezes Roger's left hand in vice-like grip. "There, there. My dream come true."

Roger squirms and grits his teeth to suppress a yelp of pain, "Eeee-owwwowch." His bobble bobbles.

"Ah, hah, there's our dwagon lady, yonder," Joe hisses, pointing toward the left front where he cleverly espies the Hamper family. "By gwosh, she is a big girl isn't she? Wonder if she's wearing a–?"

"Joe...!" admonishes Millicent.

Belinda rises and limping over to them: "Roger, Joe, I can hear your voices echoing throughout the court room. Desist!"

"That CPS solicitor, Miz Bullett, is she any good?" queries Joe, leaning forward..

"I can't get much background on the woman," whispers Belinda. "Judging from our brief encounter in the café she's a lawyer who likes to intimidate and doesn't take prisoners. Now... no moving or speaking until I give the word. Do-you-understand?"

"Not a peep, m'lady," mocks Joe.

"Keep it that way," Belinda retorts, as she leaves them to themselves and limps back to her position.

The Clerk of the Court stands up and bellows: "The Court will stand!" chattering ceases, silence. Magistrates Sir Thomas Crombie, Geoffrey Makepiece and Councillor Susan Peters solemnly enter the court room to take their seats high on the bench. The Clerk, fronting the court sits down. All follow suit. The Clerk then rises to cross the floor to confer with the Chairman of the Bench, Sir Thomas Crombie. He passes over the case notes of the day, then returns to his seat, picks up an internal phone, calling down to the cell supervisor to send up the defendant in case number one.

Before the case number one defendant appears, Belinda stands, respectfully nods toward the magistrates and approaches the Clerk's table. She asks him sotto voce to allow her colleagues to remove themselves from the public gallery to prepare, dress-wise, for case number two: Henry Osbourne.

Pre-warned, Clerk gives his all-clear. Belinda walks over to the public area and gestures for her brood to go to the nearby toilets and get changed. She returns to her place just as a uniformed policeman escorts a handcuffed, bearded man into the custodial-glass-box to the right of the court room. The Clerk focuses on the defendant and barks out routine ID questions. Answered and oath taken, Clerk bids solicitor Miz Bullett to present the Crown's case.

She rises to the occasion, "This man's crime was premeditated. He meant to steal and was caught, red-handed in the act and was apprehended. In the basket of a shopping trolley, in his possession, were three child's playthings, namely a Paddington Bear, a laptop computer and a Lego set. A patrolling police officer came upon the defendant attempting to slam a motor car's rear door shut, all this amidst a shrieking alarm. When stopped in the act and questioned, the defendant said that the playthings were in a trolley which he'd selected to take shopping, but, because a close-by car door was open, he assumed that the items belonged to the driver of that car and they had temporarily left for some unknown reason. This man says he was in the process of replacing these playthings onto the car's rear seat when the officer came upon him," Miz Bullett pauses to sip water. "So, m'luds and lady, we are asked to believe that the defendant was in the process of replacing these childs playthings on the rear seat of a motor car, purely out of the kindness of his heart? And by-the-by, undertaking this task while the motorcar's alarm was going off at a rate of 100 decibels? Hah! A totally made-up story if ever I heard one. He obviously fabricated it on the spot to explain away his theft from the said motor car. One other matter… "

Drooping eyelids from the two male magistrates indicate that Miz Bullett should get a move on.

She does, "A tyre lever… " Magistrates brighten up, a weapon? " … was also found in the trolley. The defendant claims that this was a child's toy, an imitation mechanic's tool made out of plastic. What a load of tosh! Here is said tyre lever… " Bullett's hand streaks below her small podium and reappears hefting a two-foot tyre iron. "This," Miz Bullett drops the tyre lever onto the podium with a loud clang, "is the so-called plastic toy tyre lever. No, m'luds and lady, here we have a crook, an incompetent crook at that. The charge of thieving has been proven; the defendant should receive due punishment. I submit a police report from the arresting officer who is in court to give his account of the encounter, if the defendant's solicitor so desires. I rest the Crown's case," she nods to the bench, sits down, looking around with a superior smile.

The defendant's solicitor rises to rebut the prosecution's charge. He spends two minutes explaining why his client is not guilty of the petty crime of thieving from a motor car in the town's main car park. Defendant was merely in the wrong place at the wrong time, "In fact he, being a good samaritan, was replacing said playthings, which some driver had inadvertently left unattended in a supermarket shopping trolley, into the rear seat of a motor car with its rear door wide open. He assumed the driver had been in the process of loading the car but had been called away for some reason. The car's alarm? Probably triggered by the car door being left open for some while. The tyre iron? Already in the trolley's basket when he came to wheel it away to go shopping. I reiterate my clients plea of not guilty!"

During this, barely discreetly, the newly-attired breakfast crew return and struggle into their seats. They observe that Col. Dudley Fortescue has arrived and is seated next to Sixpenny and Stanley.

"I espy a master spy in our midst," hisses Rosemary, "spying."

Joe blows a raspberry. Millicent jabs him with her elbow.

"Tanner's got him eating out of the palm of her hand," whispers Roger. "He's here to get the low-down on Henry, I'll bet. Leverage to get the old chap thrown out of Wardley."

Case one: the three magistrates retire, confer, return to declare the defendant guilty. Sentence is passed by Chairman Sir Thomas Crombie. The prisoner is led away by an immaculate white-shirted police escort.

After writing a series of notes and phoning down to the cells, the Clerk of the Court bellows: "Case number two... Henry Osbourne."

The rattling of a shopping trolley's castors disturbs the relative peace of court room number four, which is now full. A policeman trundles the trolley down the centre aisle – its sole occupant being a black brolly. He draws alongside Roger, wearing his multi-coloured head gear with bobble, and stops. The policeman sniffs, sniffs again. Roger smiles benignly at him. The policeman beats a rapid retreat.

Now, trolley quiet, eyes focus on the defendant, Henry Osbourne, being escorted into the courtroom. He is wearing a blue and white seersucker blazer with an SAS badge *Who Dares Wins* pinned on its lapel, a white shirt, smartly setting up a regimental tie; his polished pate gleams under the fluorescents. A police officer steers Henry into the custodial-glass-cage, bids him remain upstanding, facing the bench.

"He looks awfully confident, doesn't he," observes Millicent proudly.

"Yep, but he's having to bite the bullet," says Joe.

"Every bullet has its billet," retorts Roger.

"No, Woger, fate isn't part of Bewinda's plan," comes back Joe. "And by God you do pong. What–"

"It's old Tobias's trousers, they're holey too," whispers Roger.

"Used them to go to church in them did he," chuckles Millicent.

"You know what?" says Roger.

"What, pongy-pants?"

"I'm famished–" starts Roger.

"Here." Joe fishes out a crumpled packet of chocolate digestives from his cashier outfit's pocket.

Sir Thomas Crombie, having just espied a suspicious item in the aisle, beckons the Clerk to approach the bench. Their heads draw close in whispering proximity, shakes of heads and serious looks are cast in the direction of the offending wire-framed trolley with a brolly laid in it. Three pairs of eyes swing over the newly-attired breakfast squad, focussing on the multicoloured bobbled tea cosy and one over-coated, large lady. Magistrate Geoffrey Makepiece asks the Clerk, "Is this shopping trolley not being introduced into the wrong case? Did not the previous case involve a shopping trolley?" The Clerk advises Mr Makepiece that this shopping trolley is indeed relevant to case number two, and is nothing to do with case number one. Sir Thomas Crombie peers over his reading glasses, "Well, I've seen 'em abandoned on roadside verges, it's the first time I've seen one dumped in a courtroom?" Mrs Peters pops a Polo mint into her mouth while idly fingering the magistrates' guide to the 'support materials' section. Finally, and wearily, the trio assent to the defendant's use of reasonable material, but admonish the Clerk to arrest the proceedings if it becomes a pantomime. "Proceed."

The Clerk draws in a breath, momentarily visualising a cool can of beer by the pool at his favourite hotel in Bali, being waited upon by two Indonesian beauties. He licks his lips. The Clerk retreats slowly to his important place at the front of the court room where he barks out routine ID questions to Henry. Henry responds giving oath, name, date of birth, address: Wardley Officers' Residential Home, and that he is a retired government servant.

The Clerk. "The court understands and agrees defendant, Mr Henry Osbourne, will defend himself."

All eyes swivel to look at Henry.

The Clerk. "Also in court is Belinda Huxley, a retired military lawyer who will assist Henry Osbourne."

All eyes swivel to look at the now standing, acknowledging, half-bowing, smiling Belinda.

"You are acquainted with the charges against you Henry Osbourne?" Clerk addresses Henry, "They are of assault and battery upon one Lilly Hamper, and that of disturbing the peace?"

"Yes I am," replies Henry.

"Do you plead guilty or not guilty?" demands the Clerk.

"Not guilty," responds Henry.

"Proceed, if you will." The Clerk says, nodding for Miz Bullett to present the Crown's case against Henry.

Miz Bullett rises, nods to he bench and attacks without preamble, "I put it to the court that here in Henry Osbourne we have an opportunistic sexual predator who prowls the streets, shops and malls in the fair town of Plymington, forever on the lookout for the chance to accost and seduce innocent females. It is to be noted that this man's past career was as a member of MI5, and by definition, experienced in–"

Henry looks at Belinda, who nods vigorously. She yells, "Your Honour approach the bench?"

Sir Thomas nods. The Clerk shepherds both Belinda and Miz Bullett to the bench.

"This is quite outrageous," hisses Belinda, commanding the attention of at least two of the magistrates. "Osbourne's past employment has no bearing on this case, I will also point out that Miz Bullett is on dodgy ground bringing up MI5. This could lead to unwarranted publicity for Osbourne and his place of residence, and may well breach government disclosure rules in respect of terrorism laws."

"Don't be ridiculous," snaps Miz Bullett, "he is long retired, and well out of circulation in respect of his past activities. No, I cannot accept–"

"How so?" butts in Belinda. "You were about to accuse him of using his past experience in MI5 to prey on and sexually assault females."

"Miz Bullett," says Sir Thomas Crombie, "we could do without verbal theatricals from you. I will try to uncomplicate matters to the best of my ability. You will not mention or allude to MI5 again, understood? If you do so, you will incur the displeasure of this bench, and I will rule you out of order. Please stick to the rules of evidence: witnesses, police statements and such."

A miffed Miz Bullett backs away with a nod, as does Belinda. The Clerk beams at this quick resolution of a raised point of order. *Bravo!*

Miz Bullett continues, "Osbourne is a man with excessive sexual tastes, as I will now demonstrate," The prosecutor, Miz Bullett, snaps her fingers and a movie beam lights up a large screen already set up to enable all to see. "First I show the store's CCTV footage of his attack on Lilly Hamper," The film fast-forwards to people paying for their groceries in a orderly manner in a twin payment channel. A bowler-hatted Henry appears with his trolley. He turns, hangs his brolly on Lilly Hamper's backside, a melee erupts, people struggle in the aisle. Lilly Hamper, in the ensuing tug-of-war, trys to wrest the brolly from Henry, husband Frank pummells hell out of Henry, who retaliates, sparring like

Henry's Brolly

an old-fashioned pugilist. The store's security lady leaps into the frame, thrusts Henry against the counter with her elbow, half-throttling him. She is joined by a policeman and another security man. Henry is escorted away. Lilly Hamper wriggles her top down, hitches up her jeans belt, the two Hampers hug, move apart, load groceries from conveyor belt into a trolley to follow yet another security man … exit camera range.

Miz Bullett smirks as the screen goes blank, "I now bring before the court two witnesses: the cashier who saw the event and the security lady who apprehended Osbourne, to prevent his further attack on the innocent Lilly Hamper." The supermarket cashier takes to the witness stand, swears the oath. He relates that although he did see the struggle, he didn't actually see the brolly being hung on Lilly Hamper's jeans belt.

Miz Bullet frowns. This is not going to plan.

The Clerk, "Do you wish to question this witness, Mr Osbourne?"

"No, I do not."

Miz Bullett continues, "I now ask the store's security lady to give evidence."

The security lady says she was called over the alarm system to channel number seven, discovered a fight in progress, made a snap judgement as to who was the perpetrator. She points at Henry saying, "It was necessary that I use physical force to render him harmless, and then call the police."

Bullet frowns again. Somewhat better.

The Clerk: "Do you wish to question this witness Mr Osbourne?"

"No, I do not."

Miz Bullett, "Without doubt, this man will take any opportunity to molest, even, as we have seen, undress any attractive female, even in a public place. This man's audacity is astounding, his uncontrollable sexual urges, I suggest, must be curbed. Let the punishment fit the crime."

"Here endeth one totally misleading diatribe," mutters Rosemary.

"I hereby rest the prosecution's case and recommend the maximum sentence," winds up, Stella Bullett.

The Clerk stands: "So noted. Do you wish to cross-examine any of the witnesses, Mr Osbourne?"

Henry looks at Lilly and Frank 'Carver' Hamper. "No sir. I have heard and read the witness and police officer's statements. I believe my own presentation will prove me innocent of these wild accusations."

The Clerk walks over to Henry to take a proffered envelope from him, he glances at it, frowns, walks up to the bench to pass it to Sir Thomas Crombie, who flips it open, scans the revealed note and nods.

The Clerk addresses Henry, "Do you wish to make an opening speech or a closing one?"

Henry speaks, "I will open: Your worships, the police, and indeed most of us, have become concerned at the growing incidence of sexual assaults on women over the past several months in this town. This has led to, I suggest, the police and CPS being guilty of over-zealous reaction, to the point where almost any supposed assault on women in public is tenaciously pursued and prosecuted, often without dilgent investigation, as I believe to be the case in respect of myself. If the court will permit for me to be released from this custodial area, I shall be able to demonstrate what actually happened in the supermarket between Mrs Lilly and Mr Frank Hamper and myself, which was nothing more than my misplacing my broll–"

"That's a bloody lie," shouts Carver Hamper, leaping to his feet and waving his arms.

"Silence in court!" bellows the Clerk at the belligerent Frank Hamper. He looks again at the magistrates and escorting policeman. They nod, Henry is permitted to come before the bench. His alert escort stands, legs astride, arms on hips, ready to leap into action if old Henry Osbourne makes a dash for it.

Henry continues, "Although you have seen CCTV footage of the event, and while the camera identifies those involved it does not show the precise detail of what actually occurred since other people around the till area obscured certain lines of vision, hence the necessity for me to mount this demonstration." After a pause, Henry recounts the events as they happened amid constant heckling from the Hamper family and repeated admonishments for peace and quiet from the Clerk, who threatens to clear the court…

"Those are the facts, m'luds," says Henry. "And now, if I may, the demonstration," Henry nods to both Belinda and the squad. Belinda orbits the filled lawyers benches and comes up before the eager breakfast group, waving away Roger's putrid pong, holds a forefinger to pursed lips, while with her other hand waving the crew to enter the central aisle one-by-one. First up is Rosemary. The usher moves in to escort her into the central aisle.

"Oh my gawd! Take a look-at-that!" hisses Joe, nudging Millicent, in a hardly suppressed whisper. Gasps and 'oooh-aaahs' arise as lead lady, Rosemary, shrugs off her coat, and is attired, as was Lilly Hamper on that fateful day. Rosemary swings open the small gate to exit the seating area and, with the cloaked usher at her side, wobbles her way along the central aisle. The sight of such an expanse of exposed flesh, a red G-string, centred between a short tank top and low-slung jeans, causes a flurry and flutter in the court room. 'Ooohs and aaahs' continue to emanate from the public, the prosecutors, the probation service, the police and witnesses. One out-of-sight person starts a slow hand clap. But there is silence in the Wardley squad.

The Clerk bellows, "Silence in court!"

The magistrates, momentarily blind-sided, rear-view-wise, look askance at this approaching, gigantic ogre pacing, step by menacing step, in their direction, like a panzer. The usher swirls around to retreat to his place at the rear of the court room.

Joe nudges Millicent, "I detect a hint of swank, do I not?" Millicent smiles at him innocently.

"Almost steamy, not often our Rosemary sheds her thermals," chuckles Roger, rising, next up.

"You would know?" queries Joe, pinching his nose against a fresh wave of pong from Roger's pants.

"Nil commentato," rebuts Roger, standing by the small gate, ready. The usher sniffs, but moves forward.

The momentarily dumbfounded Miz Bullett recovers, leaps to her feet, her name tag bouncing over her breasts as she swings side-to-side, appealing, hands outstretched, "Approach the bench?" she yells.

The Clerk, any excuse to divert attention from this, surely a pantomime, accedes smartly to her request and bids her approach. Duty-bound, he also invites Henry and Belinda to step before the magistrates.

Miz Bullett, stony-faced, protests, "You must stop this demonstration, your worships. What on Earth can Osbourbe possibly achieve by putting on this charade, except to bring this court into disrespect? I formerly–"

Sir Thomas Crombie raises a magisterial hand. He refers to Henry's note, "In the interest of getting to the bottom of what actually happened in that supermarket …" he looks down, " … I shall permit this re-enactment, with the blessing of my colleagues. Furthermore, I suggest the Crown be less enthusiastic with their protestations and, that the Clerk shut that lot over there the hell up! Goddit?"

"Sir," begins Stella Bullett, "this chicanery must not–"

Sir Thomas Crombie points to her station in court, "Go, now!" He passes Henry's note and envelope to the Clerk, commenting. "File. Confidential." Bullett manages to glance at it in passing. It seems to be headed with a military logo, the words beneath being handwritten. *Hmmm!*

"Phew," exclaims Joe. "what a bloody palaver, and I thought it was going to be just a wegular pantomime."

Henry, Belinda and Miz Bullett return to their

Geriatricks 1

stations. Roger, poised, gets a go-ahead nod from Belinda. He removes his woolly cap to expose his bald head – as was and is Frank 'Carver' Hamper's. He collects the trolley, with brolly, and struts down the aisle wearing a soiled leather jacket, tatty jeans and blinding white trainers. En route his passage is greeted with sniffs, snuffles, coughs and handkerchiefs appearing. Out front, Rosemary body-swerves to take up her designated position in the area between the Clerk's desk and a fold-up table, representing the supermarket's checkout channel.

"Jesus H., Woger's gone quite bonkers," utters Joe in a theatrical whisper, as he too rises to his feet along with Millicent. They, escorted by a frustrated usher, follow in Rosemary and Roger's footsteps to take up their positions.

The protagonist and her husband are agog at this awesome sight. Are they seeing double? They turn and appeal to Miz Bullett, standing, shouting, gesturing, spreading their arms. She gives them a stern frown, indicates with jerky hand gestures that they calm down, and sit down, now!

Sniggers and snorts echo around the courtroom. "Silence in court," bellows the Clerk, for the umpteenth time as Millicent and Joe line up with the other two. All four now stand, prepared, waiting, ready to go.

Then, in slow motion, after being introduced by Henry, who now joins the players to enact the scene as it unfolded at the supermarket, Henry, pushing the trolley forward, stops and casually removes the brolly hooked over his arm to allow him to unload the trolley.

Henry's Brolly

He peers about myopically through his glasses. He says, "My glasses only permit limited peripheral vision, Your Honour." Then, instead of lodging the brolly on the trolley's handle, he casually hooks it onto Rosemary's exposed G-string. Roger, Rosemary and Henry then enact a three-way struggle, tugging brolly this way and that, with the resultant stretching and snapping of the G-string's band. A grin lights up Sir Thomas Crombies face. Geoffrey Makepiece adopts a serious frown, sniffing. Susan Peters says, "Air-conditioning's gorn orf I think?"

Rosemary clutches her jeans, wriggles her large bottom in a show of mock indignation, with a blowing out of cheeks and mimed invectives. Roger and Henry flail their arms and fists in a belligerent stance, in a show of fisticuffs likened to the actual show of temper by Frank Hamper. Millicent acts out a sterling performance as the security guard. She shashays up to Henry, pinning him over the table with her elbow, with Henry, hands-in-the-air acquiscent against the make-shift counter. Joe sits slumped and bored in his chair, acting as a cashier, moving his hands in slow-motion, pretending to lift groceries off of a conveyor belt and pass them by an imaginary bar-code reader, then forwarding them for packing. Not a word is spoken.

In the basin of the court Miz Bullett wears a ponderous frown as the players finish the re-enactment and shove the trolley back to rest in the central ailse, where it is collected by the usher. The breakfast squad then resume their seats to muted applause. Henry returns to the custodial glass cage, under close escort.

"That concludes my defence, m'lords," says Henry, turning and nodding to the bench, "except that I ask if may lodge with the court a paper having 98 percent of my fellow residents' and three Trustees' signatures, from the Wardley Officers' Residential Home, stating I am of good character, honest and law-abiding. I ask for this be accepted as part of my defence."

The Clerk peers at Miz Bullett, she nods, "So accepted. Cross, Miz Bullett?"

"Undoubtedly we have seen two versions of this tawdry episode. One, the CCTV footage, which I agree did not show the finer detail of the incident. The other, this so-called re-enactment, was misleading, most likely deliberately. It was nothing more than a pantomime created to misinterpret what actually did happen to the innocent Mrs Hamper." Miz Bullet shrugs, shaking her head. "The Crown cannot accept this charade to be taken as evidence. Far from it, I urge the court to disregard and dismiss what has been presented by the defendant as an irrelevant pantomime, and that it be stricken from the record."

The Clerk, rising, "I must ask the Crown to reason, to explain their motion to strike."

Miz Bullett, "Deliberately misleading, casting Lilly Hamper as a strip-tease artist. The lady was not wearing a G-string as depicted, being properly attired that day, she had no part of her rear lower back exposed. Conclusion one: Osbourne, therefore, could not have 'accidently' lodged his brolly on her exposed G-string underwear. Conclusion two: Osbourne deliberately hooked Lilly Hamper's belt in order to pull down her jeans to expose her underwear. M'luds and lady, this travesty of a re-enactment grossly misrepresents the event, it is an outrageous lie," Miz Bullett looks around triumphantly! *Put that in your pipe, Mr 'O'!*

The Clerk, "Mr Osbourne, do you wish to continue, or accept the Crown's submission that your presentation be declared irrelevant and stricken from the record?"

The 86-year-old Henry Osbourne, erect, proud, smiling almost pitifully at Stella Bullett, "Your honour and members of the bench," starts Henry. "Far from being irrelevant, my enactment exactly portrays what did go on at the cashier's outlet that day. It certainly is no misrepresentation. I can prove without any shadow of doubt that Lilly Hamper did have an inordinate amount of flesh exposed and that she wore a certain style of undergarment, which is known as a G-string. I will now–"

Sir Thomas Crombie looks at the wall clock, "Clerk, we shall recess, lunch-time. Could do with a pot of tea and a bacon sarnie," studious nods from his colleagues, who stand up and shuffle into the retiring room.

The Clerk yells, "One hour recess. Reconvene, one-thirty."

'Oooh nooo's' echo throughout the court room, people slumping back in their seats, disappointed.

Roger banters, "This is a darned sight more exciting than doling out meat balls and bacon, what?"

"We could come here evwy day, fwee entertainment. And Roger, you really must get out of those pongy pants pwonto. Oh, and take a shower at the same time. Otherwise, forget sitting with us for lunch."

"And you're too sensitive by half–"
"He's right," says Millicent. "You smell of rotten eggs."
Belinda comes up to them, "We are on a roll and, phew, Roger!" she fans her face.
"Henry performed well. More yet to come?" enquires Millicent, eagerly.
"I think we yet have a surprise or two for the beady-eyed Miz Bullett," says Belinda.
"Let's go find a place to snack. We'll send Woger in first, to be sure of a seat," says Joe.

* * *

"All stand," the Clerk shouts. The three magistrates enter and take their seats. "Court is now in session and I recall Mr Osbourne." Henry is brought into the courtroom.
He waits patiently for a quiet mement. Then, "Your Honour, I ask to approach the bench."
Miz Bullett, Belinda and Henry come before the bench. Henry looks at the Clerk, "I wish to question Lilly Hamper in private, with my friend and Crown present of course."
The Clerk gets a vigorous shake of the head from Miz Bullett. The Clerk says, "Out of order."
Sir Thomas Crombie, "Request denied."
"I was hoping to avoid embarrassing the lady, but I am afraid you leave me no choice but to prove that my enactment and statements are true and correct in all respects, before open court," says Henry.

Sir Thomas Crombie, "Mr Osbourne proceed as is your right. Go!"

They back away from the bench and resume their stations. Henry addresses the court, "To uncover the matter of bare flesh," he smiles at this, "I now inform the court that Lilly Hamper has a very large tattoo on her middle-lower back. It is a dragon breathing fire, it is some eighteen inches high. I state that I have no way of knowing the lady has such a marking on her body except for my seeing it at the supermarket on the 24th–"

"M'lords?" A riled Miz Bullett leaps to her feet. "Approach the bench?"

Sir Thomas Crombie frowns at this second interruption so soon after lunch. He looks around at his colleagues, they nod and he angles his head in assent. Again Clerk shepherds Miz Bullett, Henry and Belinda before the members of the bench.

"What … " asks Sir Thomas Crombie " … is it this time?"

"This is unprecedented," starts Miz Bullett. "We cannot have the case turning on what markings Mrs Hamper has on her body during Osbourne's sexual jostle–"

"Fossil?" Susan Peters asks, peering over her reading glasses. "Is there going to be a dig someplace?"

Sir Thomas Crombie sighs, "No, Mrs Peters, the lady before us is the CPS solicitor. She said jostle, not fossil. I urge you to focus, please."

Geoffrey Makepiece, with a glazed expression, mutters, "Why have we still got a shopping trolley in the middle of the court room?"

Geriatricks 1

Sir Thomas Crombie spreads thumb and fingers upon which he rests his brow, "It's part of Mr, oh, never mind. I want to hear from Henry Osbourne why he is revealing that he has knowledge of a big dragon tattoo on Mrs Hamper's rear, er, lower back."

"M'lord, the Crown maintains that Lilly Hamper was not in any way uncovered at the time in question, in the supermarket. If that be so, how could I possible know that the lady is so adorned? I certainly have not met, spoken, nor do I even know where Lilly Hamper lives. I'm happy to swear to this if need be. Thus by my revealing, er, disclosing that, if I may be so bold, a remarkable design over such a large area exists, I thus prove that my re-enactment was absolutely accurate, that it was merely misjudgement on my part that I inadvertently hooked my brolly on the lady's exposed underwear. So – does prosecution wish me to give this same explanation in open court?" Henry appeals to those before him.

Sir Thomas Crombie, after two minutes of thought, looks up and says: "It simply comes down to who's telling the truth; a basic question in any court of law. Who is lying and who isn't."

"If it please the bench–" urges Henry.

"No it doesn't please the bench," barks Sir Thomas Crombie. "Anyway, what is it?"

"The situation can be easily resolved by having Lilly Hamper examined by a reliable person. Then, if I am found to be right, it would seem the lady is lying about being fully covered on that day," says Henry.

"Bloody good idea," says Sir Thomas Crombie. He

looks at his colleagues for agreement, they nod. "So, Miz Bullett, do have your Lilly Hamper go somewhere private and have a trustworthy female, preferably a WPC, to see whether or not she has a dragon tattoo on her back in that specific location–"

"With the dragon's fiery breath pointing downward," adds Henry obliquely.

"With the dragon's fiery breath pointing downward," sighs Sir Thomas. "We shall now recess for fifteen minutes. I could do with a fresh cup of coffee. Go, go, go!"

"Dragon's fiery breath?" mutters Geoffrey Makepiece, peering about the court room. "I see no dragon?"

"There's at least two in the court room," says Susan Peters, "hovering."

The Clerk rolls his eyes, turns and yells, "Fifteen minute recess."

Chattering erupts throughout the court room, the magistrates are treated to cups of coffee and a surly, protesting Lilly Hamper is led away to be examined. Miz Bullett seethes and shuffles her files. Belinda, on her feet, limps over to confer with Henry, now seated in his glass cage. They talk quietly.

Roger banters, "My, what fun? How're Tanner and Stanley taking it?"

"Don't know, they've disappeared," says Rosemary.

"Probably got a whiff of Roger's pants," says Joe.

* * *

Miz Stella Bullet announces, after the court reconvenes,

"We now admit to a misunderstanding. Mr and Mrs Hamper now state that they recalled the wrong day in respect of Lilly Hamper's dress. Actually, she was indeed wearing a, er, G-string on the day in question. This was because she was due to go to–"

Henry, "I don't think it relevant we should pursue the matter of Lilly Hamper's future engagements on that day, suffice she admits exposing, however innocently, a certain item of her underwear."

"Dunno what he means," Lilly Hamper mutters, having regained her seat. "A G-string ain't underwear."

"Oh, tally-ho," chortles Joe.

"They're bellying-up," joins in Roger.

"So, they're saying that dear Henry is right?" questions Millicent.

"Spot on, Milly. He's won his case," says a cheery Joe.

Miz Bullett stands up and attempts to throw a spanner into the works: "However, we maintain that this in no way changes the situation your Honour, indeed it reinforces the issue, since the sight of this item of underwear was more than likely to arouse Osbourne's primitive urges, and goad him into launching this obscene sexual attack on Lilly Hamper's person–"

Henry: "That is a fatuous response, I move to strike."

Miz Bullett gives him a glacial look, "Not a chance."

The Clerk: "Miz Bullett, Mr Osboune, this is not a debate, desist!"

"Miz Bullett, Mr Osbourne." Sir Thomas Crombie from the bench, "do be kind enough to shut the hell up, both of you, now."

"Sir," Stella Bullett acknowledges, sitting down.

Henry nods to the judiciary: "M'lud's and lady, I hereby conclude my defence." He returns to the custodial-glass-cage with his police escort.

The three magistrates bring their heads together. Sir Thomas Crombie suggests they retire to consider the evidence presented to them in court. They agree. He waves the Clerk over, "We shall now retire to weigh the evidence. Call a short recess."

The Clerk, "You require the benefit of my considerable experience, M'lud?"

"I shall keep in mind your offer to aid us with our deliberations," replies the Chairman of the Bench.

The Clerk bellows, "Bench retiring to consider evidence. All rise," the three magistrates stand and move off into the back room to consider, cogitate, mitigate and drink more coffee – with a splash of rum.

Miz Bullett walks over to Belinda, "Your man's going down."

"Do not presume. And is it is unlike the Crown to predict a verdict?"

"Foregone conclusion. I have seen these elderly perverts sentenced time and again, community service."

"I say, let us wait and see," says Belinda.

The two ladies, stiff-faced, glare at each other. They part and resume their seats.

"Henry moved to strike, eh?" says Roger to Joe.

"Learned the law lingo, literally," Joe beams.

"Belinda is a very good teacher," says Millicent.

"Henry undertook a lot of research on his own account," says Rosemary

The Clerk addresses the court in a loud voice, "All rise," as the magistrates file in and sit down.

Sir Thomas Crombie says, "I will now pass our unanimous verdict."

The Clerk instructs, "Defendant remain standing."

All eyes are on Sir Thomas Crombie as he rises to his feet, looks around, speaks, "We find the defendant Mr Osbourne …" he puts on his reading glasses, "… NOT GUILTY on both charges!" and then quieter, leaning over, "the Clerk will record this decision and the bench's reasoning." He passes a paper to the Clerk.

Cries of jubilation from the Wardley Officers Residential Home's breakfast squad, mingle with gestures and shouts of derision from the Hamper camp.

"Order! Order!" bellows the Clerk. "We shall have order in the court!" Then the Clerk strides over to speak to Henry, "You are acquitted, you are free to go sir. But do ensure you take the trolley and brolly with you as you leave; and also that man with the pongy pants. My court room will never be the same again."

"Thank you," says Henry, nodding, "That was a proper decision by the bench, I believe."

"I am unable to comment sir. Good-day to you. Oh, the usher will bring your suitcase from the holding cell to you," says the Clerk. He pauses to once more admire Henry's lapel badge. "I salute you, sir."

Minutes pass and the court room settles down to an orderly conduct. Some make moves to leave while others reseat themselves to await possible fireworks from case number three.

The Clerk, back at his station, announces, "Mr and

Henry's Brolly

Mrs Hamper and Miz Bullett, please make your way over to me, now."

Roger nudges Millicent, "For the high jump, what?"

"Oh, why?" asks a puzzled Millicent.

"Ye'll not see 'em getting away with perjury," says Roger.

"You seem pwetty sure about that Woger," bleats Joe.

"Sure as eggs is eggs, my good fellow," banters Roger.

"Can't you bloody-well forget about breakfast?" moans Rosemary.

"Let us leave," says Millicent, getting to her feet. "We have to go and get changed."

"Nah, I like Rosemary the way she is, all togged up in that ... well," says Roger, eyeing up Rosemary.

"She is a closet nymphwomaniac you know," grins Joe.

"Will you two shut up," growls Rosemary, "before I assault you both with Henry's brolly."

"We must go and congratulate Henry," says Millicent, ignoring the ongoing banter and stepping into the aisle to join Henry and the usher pushing the trolley, now loaded with bags of re-enactment clothing, out of the court room. The others circle round as a cordon to shield Henry, should there be photographers and journalists waiting to create an unlikely celebrity.

* * *

The breakfast squad gather outside court room four exchanging excited remarks, recalling with some hilarity, various moments of their re-enactment. Joe thumps Henry on the back while Rosemary shakes Belinda's hand. "Well done, well done," they echo. No paparatzzi in evidence.

They edge through jostling crowds. Roger, pushing the trolley laden with their bundles of clothes, says, "I see stooge Stanley over yonder. Seems lost, desperate to talk to someone."

"Well, they've got a retirement home to run. Couldn't leave simple Samantha alone for too long."

"Poor man," says Millicent. "Sixpenny and Fortescue must have deserted him."

The Prosecutor Stella Bullett draws up alongside Henry, "May I say 'well done', Henry Osbourne."

"Why, thank you," he replies. "I'm flattered. You have something for me?"

"I have a case in," she looks at her dainty gold wristwatch, "half an hour ... aah, something for you?"

Henry sniffs, definitely not perfume. He gently takes her arm and guides the lady to a quieter spot under the central grove of decorative palms. "My brolly?"

Miz Bullett frowns, "You have one, in your–"

"That was for the re-enactment. My own brolly you still have. Evidence?"

"I will ensure sure that you get it back."

"And I am sure you will continue to be successful in your career. Just as I am sure you will not be in the least bit daunted by today's decision for the magistrates to find me innocent."

"A word, if you please," says Miz Bullett, looking across at the breakfast squad.

Rosemary wrinkles her nose. "Roger, that stench is still with us. Didn't you ... phew!"

"Ah, the dreaded pongy pants, in that bag there, which I will dispose of forthwith." Roger lifts the offending plastic bag from the trolley, carries over to the nearby and still-busy scanner crew, to drop it casually, unnoticed, behind their steel examination bench.

Miz Bullett looks back at Henry, her diamond-clear eyes flash. She shakes her blonde tresses about her shoulders, "Between you and Belinda Huxley you really scuppered the Crown's case. To be candid, I did not give you a chance after my closing. But, I know that something was going on in the background, and if I find out that there was any impropriety I will–"

"You, my dear, failed to properly get to the bottom of," Henry smiles, "Lilly Hamper's state of dress. It was unfortunate for you that the supermarket's CCTV camera was pointing into the store, facing the shoppers as they came forward with their trollies to unload their groceries onto the conveyor belt. This meant, on screen, Lilly Hamper, more or less, was facing the camera, so her back was unseen. Also, Frank Hamper was standing in front of his wife, even more obscuring the camera's view of her. And certainly Lilly Hamper was not going to admit she was half-dressed. Miz Bullett, you should not have shown that footage to the court. You should not have prosecuted. But you now know that now, don't you?"

"Well Henry, may I call you Henry?" she asks.

"Yes, please do," a crooked smile from Henry.

Feet away, Roger is saying to the others, "look ye yonder, our Henry, head-to-head with Bullett?"

"A lovely woman, I weally would like to get to know her, sexually," says Joe, admiring Bullett's profile.

"You mean socially," butts in Rosemary.

"Hmmm, if you say so," Joe replies, angling his head and winking.

"Shouldn't she be in court?" asks Millicent.

"Put yourself in her shoes, She want's to learn Henry's secret, how he came up trumps today."

"Beaten by an eighty-six-year oldie with nothing to gain, eh?" quips Roger. "Brilliant, what?"

"She has a reputation to maintain," says Belinda, tellingly, " and today will not help her career."

"So, she wants the low-down on Henwy's success?" asks Joe.

Miz Bullett trys to trump Henry, "Am I right in thinking your success may have benefitted from your exercising an outside influence?"

"Not so, Stella. May I call you Stella? Henry asks, not really expecting the affirmative..

"Yes, please do. But you evade my question. Influence?"

"I admit to having received some, er, coaching in respect of criminal court procedures from an expert."

"You know damned-well I don't mean Belinda whats-her-name."

"Huxley, which you know very well. Perhaps you refer to the note?"

"Yes, the note. In court, to Sir Thomas Crombie. If I find anything untoward–"

"That is twice you've referred to a sinister goings-on. Erm, haven't you another case?"

"It can wait. The note?" she almost stamps her foot.

"The note. Well, I was merely the messenger. It was from an old friend."

"I don't buy that – an old friend?"

"Greetings, one old soldier to another," says Henry with a dry smile.

Bullet changes tack, "Are they all like you at that, that, Officers' Retirement Home, superior?"

"Well, we do have a common cause, fellowship, friendship and having fun at times. Perhaps, Stella, you would consider joining us at one of our social evenings. They can be quite lively. Do please come along as my guest and join pompous, near-wealthy, stand-offish, idle, do-nothing-for-the-community bunch of old ex-military meanies in–"

"Fancy dress?"

"Ah. Not the norm. Special occasions only, my dear."

"Such as court cases?"

"Such as when we are presented with tough situations. However, I am sure that many at the home will now wish to follow your career with some interest."

"Why on Earth would they want to do that?"

"We have so much time on our hands you see," he says cynically, "it would be an exciting diversion from playing bridge, whist, snooker, bowls or golf, attending service luncheons and dinners. All so very boring. By-the-by. D'you play chess?"

"Nope. You do?" she re-slings her handbag over her left shoulder.

"Yes, county champion, three years running. It keeps one's mind alert."

"I do hope this is not your predatory instinct re-emerging, your wanting to follow my career?"

He spreads an appealing right hand, "The thought never occurred to me."

"Like hell!"

"May I take you out to dinner some evening soon?" interrupts Henry, locking eyes with the lady's.

"Hah! No doubt you already have my number?"

"And no doubt your address too," Henry grins. "Don't you know, we have our spies everywhere."

"Call me tomorrow, in the evening?"

"My pleasure. I've got to go now or I'll miss our minibus" Henry inclines his head and then, touching his forelock says, "Goodbye." He picks up his suitcase.

"Checkmate, Henry Osbourne," murmers Stella, watching him saunter away, swinging his brolley in one hand, suitcase in the other, to follow his jubilant colleagues through the main exit doors.

Outside, in front of Plymington Town Magistrate's Court, with puffy-clouds and an emerging sunshine, a joyful Joe bellows, "All aboard the Jolly Woger!" He gestures the squad to clamber aboard the minibus.

"Jolly Woger? It's always boats with you?" moans Roger as they settle into their seats.

"And it's always sex with you?" Joe retaliates.

"My attraction to the fair sex is due to my pleasant and humorous personality—"

Pearls of laughter erupt around the minibus.

Roger, po-faced, looks around, "What?"

"Can we please give up talking about sex for five minutes," complains Rosemary.

"What did I say?" bleats an indignant Roger with spread arms.

"Dear God," moans Joe Baker to nearby Millicent. "Do you think we have sufficient gwounds to claim diminishing wesponsibility?"

"You refer to Roger of course?"

"Most certainly."

"What, no Stanley?" observes Rosemary, pointedly looking around the minibus as the driver starts the motor. "Very odd he hasn't joined us."

"Already dashed orf to join Tanner, I should imagine," muses Roger.

* * *

"Where on Earth is Henry this morning?" moans Milicent, hands on hips, surveying the buffet table. She spreads her arms in an appeal to others of the squad, who are preparing to serve the queue of elderly and hungry residents milling about at the doorway.

"Never fear," bellows Rosemary with a broad grin. "Henry will be along, and he is bringing our latest recruit with him to help with our breakfast chores. And Roger, for goodness sake take orf that chef's hat, it makes you look bloody ridiculous."

"Keeps my head warm," Roger responds by flinging his head back, making the hat wobble dramatically.

"You shouldn't have started a hat twend, Woger," says Joe.

Stanley, working the toaster in Henry's absence,

leans over, whispering to Rosemary, "I don't understand what's going on?"

"Tanner has been admonished by Colonel Dudley Fortescue as I'm sure you know," she says pointedly. "The Board of Trustees were very unhappy over her negative, do-nothing attitude towards Henry in particular and the breakfast group in general. They said she was out of touch with the home's residents' activities. They were going to charge her with misconduct due to her failure to give her full support to a resident in trouble, but Henry and myself interceded on her behalf at the board meeting. We proposed simply that the Superintendent should experience what we do day-to-day, first-hand. So they relented. Carrot or stick, they gave her the option that she should participate in some of the activities and duties that residents themselves undertake, to gain insight as it were – or hand in her notice. And Henry has been invited to join the Board of Trustees as residents representative. But Stanley, I'm surprised you don't already know all this… ah, ha, here they come."

"We're here, Rosemary," announces Henry entering the breakfast room, all dolled up, ready for an early trustees meeting. At his side is Moira Sixpenny. The breakfast crew look up in mock surprise. "We have Moira with us this morning, ladies and gentlemen. She has come along to assess the breakfast squad's performance by helping out for the next few mornings. Isn't that right, Superintendent?"

A noise like a growl emits from the lady's mouth. She then asserts herself, "Yes, I'm here to do a little of what you do, to be sure that the Home's standards are being properly adhered to. Personal hygiene and food preparation and serving ability, are all part of my remit."

"Oh, do shutteth up dear lady," barks Rosemary. "We are all aware of these things, and we pay due care and attention to the rules. Anyway, it's what the Board of Trustees commanded of you, is it not?"

"Oh aye, and ye'll be serving the sloppy stuff this morning, Moira," barks Roger, pointing to a position behind the buffet table. "I expect ye'll be busy there for a while, then later on we'll get ye onto that fried stuff, bacon, meatballs and such-like," he unhooks a colourful apron, handing it to her.

"Glass of orange juice?" offers Belinda, Moira Sixpenny shakes her head.

Joe hands Moira a large ladel "Accurately placing squashy tomatoes, baked beans and mushwooms onto a wobbly plate," he smiles benignly at the lady, "is a hard nut to cwack."

"What, who got the sack?" asks Roger, adjusting his hearing aid. "Is it you-know-who?"

"Roger, shut up," growls Rosemary with a meaningful look, "and Joe concentrate on your meatballs, they are running low."

Roger raises an eyelid, "Joe's balls are… what?"

"Don't you dare!" glowers Rosemary.

"Stanley, do focus on toast quality please," says Henry, wandering, peering over his glasses. "You're very good at it but, if I may so advise, they need to be just a tad darker in colour."

Geriatricks 1

"Oh my God," utters Roger, squaring up his cock-eyed chef's hat. "This is really toooo much."

"Open the doors and let the residents in Milly m'girl," bellows Rosemary. "Let 'em all in."

Henry, brolly over arm, doffs his bowler, saying, "Good morning!" He leaves, smiling.

MADDIE'S UXB

CHARON HOUSE

Charon House, originally a 6-story Edwardian hotel, is now and since the late 1960s, a Government retirement home for senior British civil servants and those, not necessarily of British nationality, who have performed exceptional duties for Queen and Country. Charon House is located in a prime position in a well-known, and now booming, township on the Kent coast.

However, the old building's days as a retirement home are numbered. Health and Safety considerations and the lack of modern amenities are presented as the reason. Residents are advised that they will, in due course, be transferred to a Midlands country mansion recently acquired by the Authorities. The cynical say that recent planning permissions granted for the town's redevelopment will mean the old building will come under the wrecker's ball sooner rather than later. Already work is going ahead to build a giant leisure complex as part of the Town's 'New Plan'. This project, with its opening ceremony imminent will, upon completion, block off the magnificent views that residents of Charon House have of the sea, the town's esplanade, the beautiful gardens and the small harbour.

This is a bone of contention with one resident in particular.

Geriatricks 1

*At Charon House, where retired 'civvies' do dwell,
Events unravel, leading to evil Peter's death knell,
A new complex, about to deny their stunning view,
Residents, with Maddie to the fore, shout yah-boo!
Protestations ignored – work progresses at a pace,
For the stone-laying ceremony is due to take place,
But, below ground-level lurks a UXB, never found,
Maddie kills two birds with one stone – so profound.*

Madeleine leans on her stick and peers out of the fourth-floor window of the day-lounge, her eyes glow at the sight. "From here you can see France on a clear day", the care supervisors would often say, as if their words could somehow enhance their charges' rheumy eyesight. She smiles, for her France is no more than a shimmering horizon and a mélange of memories. Nearer to, she sees well enough; the English Channel sparkling under the autumn sun and a mounting breeze, a ferry jogging merrily out to sea and in the west yachts trail each other round an orange marker, heeling as they head upwind. Over the pier seagulls swoop, legs down, practising circuits and bumps on the domed theatre roof, while on the esplanade townspeople in parkas, scarves and woolly hats, parade children in pushchairs and flexi-lead their spaniels and poodles.

A sadness overcomes Maddie. She breathes in deeply to combat a surge of emotion. With the aid of her walking-stick she shuffles closer to the window to look down. Seventy feet below, between the old folks' home and the sea front, is a deep excavation, the foundations for a massive living and leisure complex.

She'd fought, written letters, even sneaked a local photographer and a high-profile journalist into the home on the pretext they were her relatives, to give them a critical interview about how detrimental the new complex would be to the fifty or so residents of Charon House. *Damn the local authority, damn so-called progress. Damn, damn, damn!*

She observes the site is being tidied up and the area around the huge hole levelled and cordoned off. Workers are busy assembling a lectern on a raised, red-carpeted, platform set back from the excavation, others are feeding a string of cables from the podium to pole-mounted speakers surrounding the area where tiers of portable seats have been set out. A uniformed police officer roams about the site, gesticulating and talking to six or seven men and women wearing fluorescent tabards. Crowd control, she assumes. *Mon Dieu!*

Maddie backs away and slumps into a chintz-covered armchair. Scowling, she peers at the wall clock: 10:35am. *Ah, soon be time for elevenses.*

She slips on her reading specs and glances down at Thursday's *Gazette*, lying on a round table beside her. The headlines shout: PRINCESS TO LAY FOUNDATION STONE AT MAMMOTH, SUPER-COMPLEX – THE PLAZA TWO-TWENTY – ON SATURDAY.

Maddie rummages in her voluminous handbag to locate a packet of cigarettes, she flips open the pack, fingers out a cigarette, places it between thin lips. An ancient silver lighter appears and she thumbs the wheel, its flickering flame is offered to the tip of the cigarette, a deep inhale and her eyes gleam with satisfaction. With the same hand, cigarette pinched between fingers, she takes up a glass of ginger wine, several sips follow. The glass is gently put down and Maddie shucks the newspaper onto her lap to set about reading the headline and story for the umpteenth time.

As she reads, a pair of blue and white trainers beneath blue jeans appear in her lowered circle of vision. She ignores them, pretending to read on. The trainers shuffle, settle into a V then the wearer sinks into the armchair next to her.

Without looking up, Maddie says, "What evil spirit did I invoke to have you sit next to me, Adolf?"

"Good morning to you too, Maddie. It's Peter, I keep telling you, Peter."

"It's that stupid moustache." Maddie then places a hand over her nose, sniffs loudly. "And, what on Earth is that awful smell. Perfume?"

"No, its aftershave. Tommy. American."

"Hah! More like tommyrot!"

He leans closer: "I came over especially to talk to you about the Superintendent's hearing on Monday."

"Hearing, what hearing." She peers at him beneath a furrowed brow.

Peter shakes his head, "You've had proper notification. Your assault, both physical and verbal, on Lady Hilda and Dolly Poyle has to be properly investigated, therefore you have to be quizzed. The Home's rules dictate as much."

"Deep interrogation, eh?" she says grimly, "Thumbscrews? Splinters under the fingernails?"

"Maddie, please," he lays a gentle, if effeminate, hand on her arm, "Routine questions. As personal care supervisor I've been asked to submit a written report for the Superintendent. Confidential of course."

"Judas," she lifts her walking stick and strikes his leg with it. "Get away from me. Go over there where I can look you straight in the eye." Maddie points a wavering stick at a chair opposite.

"I really want to help you," Peter says as he slides across into the indicated chair. "So tell me your side of the story," he flips open a notebook, a pen appears from the breast pocket of his blue shirt, poised.

"Hilda Hamden's feeble-minded and so's her crony Dolly Poyle. Put together they couldn't muster an IQ of fifty. A pound of PE up their backsides…"

"PE, Maddie?"

Maddie reaches out to flick the ash off her cigarette into a saucer, her make-shift ashtray. "For heaven's sake man, you've never heard of plastic explosive?"

"Yes, I remember that you were something or other in the services years ago. However, let us dispense with these yesteryear theatricals and get on with it."

"Don't pass me by, you young whipper-snapper, I was in secret operations let me tell you. SOE."

"SOE?"

"Special Operations Executive,"

Peter sighs, "All right, Maddie. Now then, can we make progress," his pen hovers.

"Only a dozen SOE women agents survived the war, you know."

Peter shakes his head, "Focus Maddie, please."

"Ha! Well, I found them pilfering chocolate eclairs yet again when I got to the tea trolley. I saw them wrapping five, six, maybe more into paper napkins to sneak off to their rooms. I hooked Hilda's arm with my stick to stop her. Can't have that sort of thing going on."

Peter consults previously written notes, "Lady Hilda says you came upon her like a banshee out of hell, you shouted "spread 'em wide," then you rapped inside her ankles with your stick. The nurse says she has extensive bruising and now she can barely hobble."

"Probably putting it on, looking for sympathy knowing her," Maddie inhales then, theatrically holding the cigarette away from her lips, sends out a steady stream of smoke into Peter's face.

He coughs, waving a hand. "Maddie, we've told you time and time again that smoking is prohibited in all areas, you must not… "

"She never was a pretty picture, suits her to hobble. Anyway, had to teach her a lesson. She is lucky, I can kill with my bare hands you know."

Peter scribbles a few words.

Maddie says, "I remember Dolly Poyle clawing at my arm. Had to fight her off. Write that down too."

"This isn't a one-off misdemeanour. Six written warnings for violent disruptive behaviour, plus many other incidents, all within the past two months, and your continual flouting of the non-smoking rule."

"You're a tricky one that's for sure. Pretending to be on our side, but really you're not," says Maddie.

"They may decide to send you to Room 44. It is secure and quiet there and you'll be safe from your, erm, imaginary tormentors. Although you would receive behavioural advice from a professional–"

"Hah! A bloody witchdoctor!" barks Maddie.

"No, a trained psychologist. It is a Mr Jones." Peter ignores the sarcasm.

"I won't go to that room. No way. Never," says Maddie.

"I like you, Maddie, you're a nice lady," Peter says smoothly.

"Poppycock," Maddie retorts

"We could avoid Room 44. Make it go away altogether. If… " Peter generates an ingratiating smile.

"If what?" Maddie snaps, but curious.

"It's in my humble power to influence the situation, to give you a favourable assessment, be supportive of you. To say, perhaps, you were unduly provoked."

"How does that work?" She raises an eyebrow as she stubs out her cigarette in the saucer.

"Well… a small financial gesture, something to assist me in my, say, studies."

"Studies? You? *C'est un fin*."

"I would like to tour the Pacific Islands next spring, improve my knowledge of the native culture there. I am sure that Fiji would be an excellent destination. We could call it, perhaps, an educational grant, and it would improve my chances of promotion."

"That's against the law," Maddie grips the crook of her stick, one hand over the other. "Blackmail does not work with me. I shall report you, Adolf. Be sure of that."

"Come, Maddie, let us give and take a little, you are a sophisticated and wealthy lady."

"Wealthy? Lots of money? I'm not someone you can fleece like the others?" says Maddie.

"What are you talking about?" he looks at her warily.

Maddie feels it's time mess with Adolph's mind. Her lips curl. "How is the new sport coupé Adolf?"

"Oh, it's a very nice motor" he says. "It's no secret that I've got a new one."

She slowly rotates her stick as she speaks, "A careworker with second car, a luxury soft-top at that."

"So what?"

"I was in the Secret Service, so I get to know what goes on around here. Didn't Ethel Potteridge loan you eight-hundred or a thousand a couple of months before she died? Nothing in writing I'd say, clever bugger that you are. Then there was old Jack Beer. He went off to celebrate his party in the sky leaving a sizeable bungalow in town to a man, would you believe, called Mr Brandy. What d'you make of that, Adolph?"

"You must stop these excursions into fantasy land. That's one of the reasons the others are frightened of you. Even some of our staff are wary."

"Mr Brandy wasn't a relative of Jack's, in fact no-one has ever heard of this Mr Brandy, have they?"

"Look Maddie, let us get back to my educational requirements." Peter leans forward, elbows on knees. "We shouldn't be antagonising one another like this, I am quite prepared… "

"Oh ho," Maddie chortles and taps the side of her nose. "I've got friends in interesting places. We know more than a thing or two about you, Mr Beer and Mr Brandy."

"Mr Beer was very weak, and in the end, unfortunately, he died of respiratory failure."

"Smothered himself with his own pillow, hah!" Maddie snorts.

"That's an outrageous thing to say."

Maddie sees Adolph's eyes flick side to side, "Oh

shut up, Adolph, your pious protestations are wasted on me. I was a trained interrogator. I'm not fooled."

Peter shakes his head, waves the notebook, "I've spoken to other residents who verify what Miss Poyle and Hamden reported as accurate. But their comments are, at present, confined to this notebook, if you convince me there may be circumstances that might change matters… "

"Seven-hundred and fifty thousand that bungalow was worth. Why ask me for a so-called grant?"

"Stop right there. This is intolerable. I shall have to report you," Peter says.

"You're as crooked as a donkey's hind leg."

"You don't have any relatives that we can contact, do you?" says Peter, creating a broad cynical smile.

"Not living I don't. But I do have a number who are dead."

At that moment a group of elderly residents straggle into the day-lounge. Dolly in the lead, Lady Hilda following; she is limping, using a walking stick. The two women nudge each other when they see Peter, sat across from Madeleine, notebook in hand.

Maddie glares at them. "Traitors," she shouts.

The two old ladies scurry across the day-lounge to perch in their favourite chairs to await the morning tea trolley. The others also find seats, chattering among themselves. Morning newspapers are unfolded as they seek to understand the headlines and study pictures of the famous and their latest escapades.

"See what I mean?" Peter says. "They're frightened of you."

"Adolph, you're a fool. And so am I… too ancient to care probably."

"It's Peter," he sighs. "Well, I really can't have you repeating these half-baked stories to Superintendent Hermitage on Monday. It would be quite inappropriate."

She says, "You should be more worried about the meeting to be held on Tuesday. It will be of some considerable importance to you."

"You misunderstand, Maddie. Your interview is on Monday."

"Not my meeting, yours."

"Mine? You've got it all wrong."

"No I haven't. On Tuesday it will be your turn to be interrogated!"

"I haven't the faintest idea what you're talking about. I've heard nothing about… "

"It's all over for you Adoph. Through my… " Maddie again taps the side of her nose, "… contacts, I got to see your bank account. Very interesting reading, all those big credit payments over the past two years, well in excess of your salary."

"You're out of your mind! This is sheer fantasy. A fairy story. And, how dare you… " he splutters into silence, running his mind over this revelation. *The old lady has rumbled him. She'll have to go.*

Maddie waits while Peter thinks it over before she hits him with another low blow. "So, at my request Superintendent Hermitage approached the local CID. He agreed something was seriously wrong. I don't know, Adolph, you're the brightest young man I've met in a long time. Why you should choose to work with sedentary, senile and frankly bad-tempered, rude, feeble, old folk is beyond me. I suppose there is always room for the criminally-minded, even in an old folks home. Sooner or later I knew you would put a foot wrong; a half dozen years inside should straighten you out though."

"What bank?" he says suddenly. He finger-flips his notebook shut, pen shoved into his shirt pocket.

"Huh?"

"You said about a bank, my bank. So, what bank?"

"Winterbournes, in the High Street." Maddie smiles. "You see, I know everything."

"Rubbish. I bank, erm, elsewhere, certainly not at Winterbournes."

"My contacts are with professional people. They and I know where you bank."

"You're suffering delusions. I may have to call Nurse to sedate you."

"Stop my meeting on Monday with the Superintendent, and I'll stop yours on Tuesday with the CID. I have influence."

"Another charade. These figments of the imagination must stop, Maddie."

"I'll spill the beans. Watch me."

"You'd be making a big mistake. The Superintendent won't entertain tittle-tattle about staff, especially if it comes from a senile, over-ninety crone such as yourself, with your reputation."

Maddie sniffs. "Insulting me won't change anything," She lights up another cigarette.

Peter says, "Well if that's the way you want it. My

assessment will be impartial, although in view of your extremely negative attitude I shall be unable to report your side of events in as good a light as I otherwise might have done. It's looking likely that I'll have to have you be placed in Room 44 pending your interview."

"I'll tell them all about you."

"Oh! I don't think so, not with you being, er, absent," he snarls.

Maddie is startled at his vehemence. "Room 44 is an isolation room, hmm?" she says, knowingly.

"Yes it is. And clients are monitored by the hour and so are under the closest supervision."

"Incarceration if you ask me," says Maddie.

"Look here Madeleine, this is a pleasant home for retired civil servants, albeit we're a mite over-numbered these days. Living longer and all that. But nevertheless we care for all our clients equally, humanely and with due propriety." Peter smiles at this well-used mantra.

"A pleasant home? With that horrible building soon to overshadow us, and over-numbered? We'd be better off if we jumped from the balcony with ropes, and I don't mean bungees, tied to our ankles. We'd go over in pairs *la danse macabre*, heh, heh! You could empty this place in an afternoon. Make a bloody mess on the side of the building though. Might even shock some sense into those darned construction managers outside. Half a dozen dangling bloodied bodies should stop 'em in their tracks." Maddie gestures to the balcony overlooking the sea, the esplanade and the construction site.

"You keep clear of that balcony, it is forbidden for residents to go out there, as is repeatedly explained to all of you during our weekly meetings. It's very dangerous for old folk," warns Peter.

"We shouldn't be in an old building like this, stuck four stories up in the air. We should all be living in the countryside with the birds, the trees, shrubs, beautiful lawns, ponds with ducks, swans, moorhens..."

"So be it Maddie," he murmurs. "There are plans for the home to move in a couple of years or so when finance permits."

"Not in my lifetime," she retorts.

"That brings up another matter, also on Monday's agenda."

"Agenda? Oh, how official," Maddie says, with mock haughtiness.

"It's serious. Your voluble, wordy, written objections to the Town Hall about the new complex, which incidentally breaks all the house-rules, by-passing the Superintendent, management and trustees. And that awful interview with the press and independent television people; utterly outrageous. Myself, the staff, the Superintendent, were astonished you would turn on the very people who love and care for you so diligently and sincerely."

"You, love? You, care? You, diligent? Hah!"

"We shall be largely unaffected by the construction of the Plaza Two-Twenty complex. Perhaps some small inconvenience during the construction period, no more," explains Peter.

"I'll never see the sea or the sky again when that monstrosity is put up, all I'll see is a brick wall, you and that horrible bunch sat over there. You, the management and trustees have," she stabs a finger at him, "failed me and my friends totally. You're all cowards, a plague on you!"

"Charon House's governors have worked closely with the town planners in an effort to keep disturbance to a minimum, but they also explain that the complex will be for the future benefit of the whole of the local population."

"Fiddlesticks, it's damn-all good for us elderly residents, stuck in here… "

"Just now you wanted them all to commit hara-kiri."

"Adolf, you're too tricky for your own good," she stubs out her cigarette-end, picks up her glasses, snaps them on and begins to read, ignoring him completely.

After a prickly silence, he gets up abruptly and stalks out of the day-lounge.

* * *

Down on the Plaza Two-Twenty construction site, between Charon House and the esplanade gardens, preparations for the foundation stone laying ceremony are approaching fever pitch. Deep in the bowels of the forty-foot excavation, officials wearing hard-hats and armed with clipboards, plans and papers, gather in groups, nodding and pointing at crane drivers high up in their cabs and sign-marked locations nearby. At ground level, workmen pull strings of red, white and blue bunting out of boxes to fix them around the temporary stage, their mates rolling out a royal blue carpet leading to the podium. Others are busy around

Geriatricks 1

a flagpole raising a Union Jack alongside the corporate flag. Across the three-acre site, behind dozens of rows of fold-up metal chairs, a TV crew climb into a crow's nest on a scaffold frame to erect their cameras.

10:50am. Earle Kingston, the town's Chief Executive, leans on another scaffold cat-walk rail, overlooking the site, watching the men at work. His department's job of organising the ceremony after several months of preparation is almost finished. Except to receive the dignitaries, a minor Royal, the new Mayor, a select number local councillors and VIPs, there is little else to do. All of them invited because of the importance to the area of the new complex. Twenty-two stories of luxurious community living, extensive business suites, six shopping levels, a sky-top revolving restaurant, a health spa, a leisure centre, an Olympic size swimming pool, a gymnasium and underground parking for hundreds of vehicles.

Clive Magog, the construction manager, climbs up to stand alongside Kingston. "Lucky you. Nothing to do?" he says, puffing hard.

"From here on Magog, I'm leaving it to your experts. I have just got to introduce the Mayor to his Royal guest, then," he spreads his hands wide, "sit back and watch. Tell me, what is this special demo I've been hearing so much about?" asks Kingston.

"Right. At one o'clock sharp, after the speeches, we'll punch the first three of eighty steel piles into the ground on which the whole complex will eventually sit. You see those long-jibbed cranes?" Magog points.

"Yeees," Kingston says, looking across at the giant crawler units positioned around the excavation.

Maddie's UXB

"Suspended from each is a pile-driving rig which hammers the columns sixty-feet into the ground. It will be quite a sight, and sound too, engines roaring, piles being hammered in, all while the band plays."

Clive Magog looks across at the face of the brick four-story building. "I don't fancy those old folk in Charon House will be too happy when the pile driving gets going. It'll be noisy, the ground will vibrate, and it will go on for weeks. Still, they've been told what to expect."

"They'll get a good view of today's opening ceremony at least. Grandstand seats," grins Kingston.

"For today, and until the building's finished. But then, I'm afraid, they'll be facing a concrete wall."

* * *

As Maddie reads the paper a sudden chill envelopes her, the hairs on the nape of her neck prickle and a shiver ripples through her body. She draws the lace shawl tightly around her hunched shoulders, pecks her dress over her knees and bickers to herself about Charon House's heating system. It is suddenly very cold, icy cold even. *Yet it was warm barely a few minutes ago?*

"Madeleine? Madeleine Treadwell-Bennett?" A voice interrupts Maddie's muttering, she looks up, she becomes aware of a soldier sitting in the chair just vacated by Adolf. *Where on earth has he materialised from? They're all at it; creeping up on you in fancy dress, shouting in your ear: Do this, do that, go here, go there. Bossy bloody lot. Don't recognise this one though?*

"Yes, young man. I am she," she says warily.

"I'm Freddy Fowler, Madeleine. Corporal Fowler, Royal Engineers, Bomb Disposal, Twelve Squadron." He wears a khaki uniform and incredibly he is holding a tin helmet over an old war-time gas-mask on his lap, and yes, good old army boots too. She smells brick dust, burnt timber, and something else. Maddie's memory spins excitedly. *Yes – the smell of explosive!* She stares at him, eyes wide.

"Goodness, are we being attacked?"

"No, Madeleine," he holds up one hand. "Do not be alarmed. May I call you Madeleine?"

"Yes, all right. But what's happening? Why are you wearing that old army uniform?"

"I'm here to talk especially to you," says Corporal Fowler.

"Hah. That's Adolph's opening line," Maddie says, sarcastically.

"Adolph?" he queries.

"It's a long story," she sees that his battledress is ripped and blackened in places and blood-stained. She looks at his knuckles, badly grazed, bloody, a dirty bandage binds his right hand and his fingernails are dirty, ripped and torn, he is unshaven. *What a disgraceful state for a soldier to be in.*

"I'll call Nurse immediately," she says, making to rise to go and ring the bell, expecting him to say no.

So he does, "no Madeleine, I'm not hurting, really."

She looks into his eyes. True, she sees no pain, but something else, a light shines from within. Maddie fondles the little gold cross at her throat. It's warmer now, at least.

"We don't have very much time. I have come to ask for your help," the soldier says.

She smiles sweetly but espies the time on the wall clock, nearly eleven. *Tea, cakes and scones are due.*

"During the evening of August 24th in 1940," he begins, "a stick of twelve 250kg bombs were dropped by an enemy bomber along the High Street. Eight or nine went off, but three or four didn't – we thought it possible they could be delayed-action types, a well-established terror tactic. All hell was breaking loose, fires, explosions, burst water mains, people stumbling out of houses, crying out, ambulances, fire engines trying to get through piles of rubble. Anyway, we got our plot line worked out as to where the bombs had fallen, and identified possible unexploded bombs..."

Madeleine looks round as a staff lady pushes the tea trolley, rattling, into the lounge.

"... I decided to disarm a UXB next to the Rex cinema first. I couldn't wait for Lieutenant James as he was busy with another UXB up at the Mount. It could only be a matter of time before our bomb went off, delayed action meant anything from five minutes to three days, even longer. No way to know."

"Oh, I know. I remember in France, near Toulouse, Marcel Robards, Monique and I went to blow up a railway bridge, and we too couldn't..."

Hilda, Dolly and others grasp chair arms to help climb to their feet and painstakingly negotiate a route around tables and chairs, heading for the refreshment trolley. They pause and stare at Maddie. "Who on earth are you talking to? Yourself?" Hilda cackles.

"Not planning another attack are you?" smirks Dolly.

"The Superintendant will send you to room 44 if you do," hisses Hilda.

Maddie wants them to hear her new companion: "Continue, Corporal, what happened next?"

"I went through the routine, by the book. Stood my sappers clear, checked and double checked, but I sensed this one was different, it had a new type anti-personnel device fitted, mercury, made to look like a standard fuse, and then, boom!" he studies his hands.

Maddie raises her voice, speaking to Hilda and Dolly: "I'm listening to Corporal Fowler, you too should be listening, he's talking about the bombs dropped here during the war."

"She's crazy," sneers Dolly. "Bombs?"

"Dolly," Hilda says gleefully, "we must report this to Peter right away."

Maddie realises they can't hear Corporal Fowler, then it dawns on her that they can't see him either. It's as if he's invisible to them.

"I shouldn't have hit you, Hilda Hamden..." Maddie starts.

"No you shouldn't," Hilda replies, "I've got bruises and..."

"... I should have killed you," she barks.

The two old ladies clump away, looking anxiously over their shoulders.

Freddy Fowler goes on, "I lost it. Boom! That was the end."

"Corporal, I'm not being disrespectful, but it is time for our morning cup of tea," she looks across the room anxiously. "I'll bring you a cup over. Do you take sugar? Do you like scones? Occasionally we have strawberry jam, and cream too."

"By midday," he says urgently to her face, "it will be too late to do anything."

"You will have to be patient for a few more minutes, young man. I will listen to your story when I come back, those vultures will pick the plates clean in no time. I have to be constantly vigilant you know."

She grasps her stick, stands awkwardly, turns, starts off toward the chattering group at the tea trolley.

He says to her back, "Madame Madeleine Girronde, Croix de Guerre, Légion d'Honneur, MBE."

She stops, turns round slowly. "You seem to know more about me than most, Corporal."

"Madeleine, we have an urgent task before us. You see, there is one live 250kg bomb buried under the construction site in front of Charon House. They never found it that night… it's still there!"

Maddie returns, slowly sits down, tea and cakes forgotten.

* * *

"Sergeant Warren, Mill Lane Police Station, speaking."

"Hello? This is Madeleine speaking," her voice reedy

on the phone. "I am calling from Charon House, it is the retirement home near the sea front. You would know it I think?"

"Yes madam I do, and what can I do for you?" asks Sergeant Warren.

"I am reporting an unexploded bomb at the building site in front of us. You must do something about it quickly, there is to be an important event to be held there very soon," she explains.

"I see, Madam."

"It's Maddie," she smiles sweetly at the corporal standing next to her.

"Well, er, Maddie," Sergeant Warren says gently, "do you live at Charon House, and why would you think there is a unexploded bomb on the building site?"

"Yes I do live here, if you can call it that. However, there isn't much time."

"Maddie, your full name please."

"Madeleine Treadwell-Bennett."

"And what can you tell me about this, er, bomb?"

"I'm told that there is a big ceremony at one o'clock and after that I understand that the construction machinery will start working. There will be lots of people gathered around, some very important people: the Queen's cousin I believe, the Mayor and, oh dear, dozens of others. You must stop it, those machines will very likely set the bomb off."

"I'll report it straight away, don't you fear," he says, mildly alarmed.

"Thank you, Sergeant. Oh dear, oh dear, I'm all of a shake. Goodbye."

"Hold on Mrs Treadwell-Bennett, who was it that told you about the..."

Madeleine hangs up the phone. "Come along, Corporal Fowler," she says. "We'll go onto the balcony. It overlooks the building site and we shall see the police clearing the area, and find the bomb," taking his arm, she holds herself erect. "Forward soldiers, into action."

They step out proudly, through the day-lounge, past slurping, hunched-up old-timers. When they get to the balcony door Maddie pauses, "I will need the key, young man, to open this door."

"It's kept locked?" he queries.

"Forbidden territory to us ancient ones, they think we'll fall over. Although I'm sure that one or two here deserve a push. Perhaps that's why... "

"Where is the key, Madeleine?"

Maddie looks vague, shrugs, "I suppose, yes, its kept in the Superintendent's office."

The Corporal strides away. Moments later he's back with the key dangling from a red wooden ball.

"Yes, that's it," Madeleine unlocks and pushes the door open. They step into full sunlight and stand, side-by-side, leaning on the parapet. They look down.

"There's no sign of an evacuation I fear, it's still very busy down there," observes the Corporal.

"*Sacré bleu!* They continue to come into the area. The Sergeant said he would take immediate action."

"It'll take a little longer for the message to get through, Madeleine. But when it does you'll see the police move the workers and people out quickly enough. Then they'll check the town hall's records to

Geriatricks 1

locate the exact position where that bomb is. You see, in the war all bombs were plotted and charted, so later on the Army would know where to dig for any UXBs."

"But they didn't dig up this one. I wonder why not," Maddie queries.

They study the scene below for signs of a change in behaviour.

"I don't know," he answers.

"It must be nearly eleven-thirty. Something's wrong, I can feel it." Maddie shivers, even in the sunlight.

"Be patient; good old boys them coppers," says the Corporal.

"Look, I do believe... yes, they're stopping them at the entrance now."

* * *

Construction manager Clive Magog threads through the bandsmen, site workers and officials and then climbs onto the stage. "I've been passed a very important message," he whispers to the town's Chief Executive Earle Kingston, who is surveying the activity, "from that police officer over there." He nods towards the uniformed police officer herding his security team into a line-up.

"Well, what is it man?" Earle Kingston anxiously consults his watch: Eleven-thirty-five.

"He says there's an unexploded bomb on this site. Work must cease immediately, we must evacuate."

"Good God!" Kingston exclaims. "This is damned serious. But we've had no reports of terrorist groups or nut cases. This is an urban project for Christ's sake, nothing to do with ruining the environment or polluting it. We absolutely must commence the unveiling ceremony at one o'clock, as planned."

"The policeman is adamant," Magog insists.

"The Mayor is en route," the Chief Executive barks, "the Royal entourage is due within the hour. I don't believe it." He marches off the stage and strides up to the uniformed police superintendent in charge.

"Look here officer," he growls.

"Inspector Bloom, sir. And whom am I speaking to?"

"What's this about an unexploded bomb?" demands Kingston. *He knows bloody-well who I am.*

"Calm down sir. Don't let us get in a panic. My people will stop anyone coming in, and we will start to evacuate the site, if we have to. Quietly and without any fuss or panic. I must also alert the old folks' home, Charon House, which we will also have to evacuate," advises Inspector Bloom.

"I can't let you do this," says an angry Kingston.

"Really, sir?" he looks at Kingston with raised eyebrows.

"I need more information. It's vital we proceed, some VIPs are already here for the ceremony, and the Royal party is due at… "

"Then we shall have to divert the Royal party to a safe area sir, and with your influence and charm, get the Mayor and everybody else to keep clear and perhaps circle around for a while. I will let you know when … " he smiles at his upcoming pun, "… the coast is clear."

"That is not good enough," replies Kingston sourly, "I can't cancel the event on one man's say-so, with respect Inspector. I mean, is it a terrorist threat? Where is the bloody thing? And," his voice cracks, "is it due to go off?"

Bloom considers, says, "My instructions from the Commander is to get the site cleared of people, also Charon House. Top priority. Standard procedure when we get a bomb scare. The bomb squad are on their way and will be here within minutes to conduct a search and defuse the thing, if there is one. But I'll get more information to you as the situation unfolds," he says, repeating himself.

The Chief Executive shakes his head in dismay.

Bloom speaks into his mobile. It responds immediately. He says to Kingston, "Apparently there was a phone call informing the local station desk Sergeant that an unexploded world-war two bomb is buried under the construction site."

"How the hell would anyone know that?" asks Kingston, wearily. "And just as we are about to launch the opening ceremony?"

"They're rechecking the source now, sir.

"Madeleine Treadwell-Bennett at Charon House," squawks the voice over the phone.

"Madeleine Treadwell-Bennett at Charon House?" repeats the Inspector Bloom.

"Madeleine Treadwell-Bennett," yells the Chief Executive, overhearing, "I don't bloody-well believe it."

"You know the lady, sir?" Inspector Bloom stares hard at Kingston, wearing a inquiring smile.

"I'll say I do. An awful woman. She's almost single-handedly opposed this project, tooth and claw, from the start. You've no idea the trouble she has caused. I tell you Inspector, this is a ploy, a mean, cruel trick by an embittered old lady determined to stop this ceremony going ahead by any means."

Bloom turns away to speak into his mobile. He nods, says to Kingston, "I've got two officers going into Charon House now sir. If it's a hoax they'll get to the bottom of it pronto," he checks the time, 11:45am. "I'll give them ten minutes, fifteen max."

The Chief Executive nods grimly.

* * *

Two uniformed police officers, kit abounding their bodies, storm into the day-lounge. Residents gasp as the two, a male and a female, move about the room, asking the whereabouts of one Madeleine Treadwell-Bennett. "Where is she?" demands Constable Bates, appealing to all.

Several trembling fingers point towards the balcony. The two officers dash out onto the balcony and stop at the sight of old Maddie leaning on the parapet.

"This little old lady, making hoax calls?" queries Constable Bates to his partner.

"We saw her at the telephone," says Hilda, shuffling up behind them.

"Heard her say something about a bomb," Dolly chants, at Hilda's shoulder.

Geriatricks 1

"I will confirm that," says Peter, poking his head round the door.

"Madam," Constable Bates addresses Maddie formally. "Was it yourself that called the police a short time ago to report a bomb threat?"

"Yes Officer, I did. But it is no idle threat, there is an unexploded bomb down there. I understand it will go off if that machinery starts pounding the earth," Maddie replies.

"How do you know this?" asks WPC James.

"This young Royal Engineer Corporal told me all about it," she indicates Corporal Fowler next to her.

"Who?"

"Tell them, Corporal." Maddie beseeches.

The Corporal starts speaking… but Maddie sees that they can't hear him and suspects, as with Hilda and Dolly, that they can't see him either. Police Officer Bates looks at Maddie oddly for a long moment.

Bates signals his companion, WPC James, to watch over Maddie. Then he urgently ushers Hilda and Dolly out of the crowded balcony and into the day-lounge.

Through the doorway Maddie sees him talking earnestly to Adolf then, after a while, to both Hilda and Dolly, who point in her direction. PC Bates speaks into the radio at his shoulder, his eyes meeting with hers.

* * *

"The Commander has given the all-clear, sir," Inspector Bloom relays to Kingston, "after giving all due consideration to the circumstances, well, you know. So, the ceremony may proceed as planned."

"The old bat should be locked in a mental institution." Kingston turns to Magog, standing beside him. "Clive, carry on. With luck we should finish the speeches by half-past one. Then it's all yours, for the big demonstration. I could murder a stiff drink."

* * *

Peter sidles onto the balcony, hovering next to WPC James, away from Maddie. "What is going to happen now, Officer?"

"Hard to say, sir, but I think they'll carry on with the ceremony," says WPC James.

"I mean to Maddie here?" presses Peter.

PC Bates appears, overhears, "We'll leave her to you people. A thorough ticking-off should do it. But I advise you and your staff to remain vigilant while the work is going on. Know what I mean?"

"I don't think she will be here much longer," Peter mutters.

"Did you say, they'll carry on, officer?" interrupts Maddie.

"Maddie, you've caused enough trouble for one day," says Peter. "Now come inside. Come."

Maddie leans over the parapet and looks down at the site. She gasps: "I don't believe it. They're letting them in again. Those poor people. They mustn't. What is the time please?"

WPC James responds, "It's twelve o'clock."

Maddie lifts her head and looks out to sea for a long moment. *Perhaps to see her beloved France.* Finally, she says, "It's time for us to do our duty, Adolf."

"Adolf, who the devil's Adolf?" asks PC Bates, looking round, bewildered.

"It's her pet name for me," growls Peter as he grips Maddie's arm.

"*Adieu*, Corporal Fowler," Maddie says, looking sideways.

"A*u revoir Madeleine,*" Corporal Fowler replies gently, with a smile.

PC Bates and WPC James step aside to let the old lady and Peter pass to go inside.

But Maddie doesn't move. "Now, Adolf," she say, "we must experience the real meaning of sacrifice."

Peter frowns, "Sacrifice?"

She takes up her walking stick, turns around and throws it in a spinning arc over the construction site. The onlookers smile, puzzled, inching forward to watch it drop to the ground.

While they are distracted Maddie turns her back to the parapet, and suddenly wraps her arms around Peter's neck, locking her hands. She throws herself backward, his body is jerked forward with her weight, they tumble against the parapet. Desperately Adolph thrusts out his hands, off-balance. Maddie pulls harder, they teeter on the lip of the parapet in a macabre embrace.

The officers leap forward, reach out... too late. The two figures topple over. Peter's eyes pin-ball with terror, his mouth gapes wide, he shrieks. Maddie smiles, tightening her grip. Her shawl streaming out like a failed parachute as the pair plummet to the ground.

* * *

It is a wet, overcast, Monday morning and Clive Magog stands on the cat-walk at the construction site, staring down. Below, on the edge of the excavation hole, army sappers slip and struggle to erect a heavy-lift gyn over a muddy hole. Nearby men and women in white one-piece suits and police officers huddle in a group talking and studying plans.

Magog frowns, remembering Saturday. Immediately after the death plunge, they had closed and cleared the site. The bodies of Madeleine Treadwell-Bennett and Care Home Supervisor Peter Ayckbourn had been removed after an examination by police officers. On Sunday he had come in to brief his engineers for an early Monday start, only to find the site still under the control of the Police and the Bomb Disposal experts. They were scanning the whole area with hi-tech X-Ray equipment. Earle Kingston had been there carrying some old town charts, and had told him that until the experts were finished the site would remain closed.

He leans on the rail, padded jacket zipped up, idly flapping Monday's *Southern Telegraph* against the palm of his hand. It is folded to expose the headline, SUICIDE STOPS CEREMONY. PRINCESS, MAYOR, SHOCKED! Sub-heading. Hero. Home Care Supervisor killed trying to prevent deranged resident from committing suicide.

Magog watches a limousine splash into the area. Kingston climbs out, pulls up his collar, strides over to the police group. They get into a huddle, then a white suited officer lays something in the Chief Executive's hand. Kingston peers closely at the objects before handing them back. He nods thank-you and moves away, looking up to see the construction manager. He waves and beckons to him. Magog starts down. They meet in a circle of puddles.

"Sorry about this, Magog," the Chief Executive says, "they say they'll be finished tomorrow sometime."

"Head Office is furious, we're falling way behind. The old lady's suicide and the man's death are turning into a PR disaster for my company, and have you seen this," he waves the newspaper.

Kingston retorts: "Don't your people understand? It was almost a national disaster. It could well have read: 'Royals, VIPs, dozens killed by a wartime bomb'. We're damned lucky to be alive, thanks to that old lady. One very special old lady."

Magog asks, "So, tell me Earle, how did they make the connection from the death plunge of those two unfortunates from Charon House to the discovery of an unexploded bomb? I mean to say, aside from the old lady's bomb threat, which was dismissed by the police, there was little reason to... "

"Eagle-eyes over there," Kingston interrupts, and nods toward Inspector Bloom. "He was first to get to the bodies. The two were quite dead, obviously. But they'd fallen onto the grass perimeter beside a privet hedge, barely a dozen feet from the old folks' home. The old lady's right arm was flung out and in her open palm was a corroded metal disc. Bloom tried to pick it up, but found it attached to a cord threaded through her fingers, this was itself buried in the ground under the hedge. He carefully pulled it out and he found a second disc attached to the cord. A pretty mucky state too, he said. Turned out, when he looked at it closely, that they were military ID tags."

"ID tags?"

"Dog tags, the Americans call them. All war-time service personnel wore them round their necks."

"Yes, I know that," retorts Magog.

"Do you believe in ghosts Magog?" asks Kingston.

"Why?"

"Earlier, I was with the police at Charon House. We couldn't understand how the old lady could have known about a bomb, a UXB, buried on the site. We still don't know. But those in the day-lounge said that during the time before she and the care worker went over the parapet, she had been talking to a soldier, an invisible soldier, because nobody else saw him… "

"A invisible soldier?"

"Yes. The old lady addressed him as Corporal Fowler."

"Okay. So?" Magog frowns.

"The ID tags in the old lady's hand were found to be those of none other than one Corporal F. Fowler."

"Good God! But that still doesn't explain what led them to search for a bomb? Finding an soldier's ID tags wouldn't in themselves have been… "

"Inspector Bloom had stopped, as you know, all proceedings following the demise of those two people."

"Quite right too."

"Bloom told me that the bomb scare by the old lady, ID tags identifying a bomb disposal soldier from the war, and what with a bomb squad already on site, gave him vibes – policemen call it gut instinct. So he ordered a detailed examination of the whole construction site. First of all they found human bones just outside the hedgerow, a couple of feet down, then they discovered a bomb some two-hundred yards away, just below the surface, near the edge of the excavation. It's a miracle it hadn't already been struck by a back-hoe or a dozer blade during the preliminary excavation work." Kingston spreads his hands wide.

"But those charts you had. Didn't they indicate where the bombs had fallen in the war?"

"No. Although well marked, they only show the UXBs accounted for."

It starts to rain. Kingston tilts his head, says cheerio and starts to climb into his limousine.

Magog, holding the door, says, "I see the home supervisor chappie is being labelled a hero."

"But he wasn't. He was apparently in serious trouble for certain irregularities at Charon House, what they might be I don't know. I have been told that the police are trawling Criminal Bureau Records. Their investigation of the man continues apace."

"A bad seed, eh?"

"He certainly wasn't the knight in shining armour as depicted in the Press. That sobriquet should be worn by one Madeleine Treadwell-Bennett. Yes?"

Magog nods agreement.

Kingston slams the door, lowering the window. "Oh, by the way Magog… "

"Yes?"

"The complex is to be renamed the Treadwell-Bennett Centre."

"I hope she finds the view to her liking. From the top she should be able to see France on a clear day."

"If not," Kingston chuckles, "watch out."

"*Touché!*"

TOBIAS' CATTLE

TOBIAS PEABODY'S HIGHLAND HERD

"Farming ain't what it used to be," old Tobias Peabody would frequently say, over a pint of bitter at the Shoulder of Mutton. Himself, wife Mildred, and their two sons, Jonathan and David, Tobias' partner, with the help of part-time labour, work all hours, all seasons, in all weather, to keep their Wiltshire farm afloat financially.

Then ... Tobias' highland herd attracts the attention of a film company, G.E.M.Pix, based in Craxton, near Swindon, who are in the process of making a blockbuster movie. The movie script calls for scenes showing a highland cattle stampede. They eventually trace the only highland herd in the west country to Tobias Peabody's farm. This led to their outdoor film experts arriving unannounced at old Tobias' door, to ask him if they could film his highland herd – for a fee.

They agree a fee after a protracted negotiation. Outcome: Peabody's are pleased, if not ecstatic. The film crew are happy, and get to work filming the relevant cattle scenes. Old Tobias and Mildred sit back to await their reward for the 'use of', in the form of cheque payment.

Geriatricks 1

One morning providence offers Tobias a pot of gold,
The movie men tempt him... so will he be so bold?
With shenanigans and a sigh old Tobias does agree,
They to digitise his highland herd, for a decent fee,
All done, as soon as blink, he bills their money guy,
Then: Ha, ha, a mirthless cackle echoes o'er the sky,
Hanky-panky now in play, will there be no reward?
Protests ignored: so Tobias puts them to the sword.

Tobias firmly pats the hind quarters of Charlotte, one of their four pregnant Guernsey cows. She, unperturbed, continues munching a mouthful of hay. Tobias says to his wife, standing close by him in the cow shed, "Signs are the old girl will be dropping soon Mildred, like sometime tomorrow."

"Right you are. I'll phone the vet, warn him. Though I do hear he's overworked of late," says Mildred.

"Good business these days," Tobias slides his hand down Charlotte's swollen abdomen, kneels, feeling the weight of her udder. "Do believe they be better off than we farmers–" he stops talking and looks up. "What's that?"

Mildred says, "I hear a motor. We got some folk come a visitin'?"

Tobias looks through the half-open barn door, over the yard's low stone wall toward their thatched farmhouse, bathed in late spring sunlight. "Visitors to be sure. It'll be them DEFRA or Health and Safety officers I shouldn't wonder. Never let us be these days. Always poking, prodding around, yard, barn, meadow. They come checking the stock, soil, whatever takes their fancy, seems to me."

"Doubt it's them. This looks a real nice vehicle; not their usual rusty, dusty, one. This one's all shiny, well, under all that streaky mud," observes Mildred.

Tobias peers – eyesight held up good at last week's eye test, still only needing reading glasses. "I see what you mean. Looks like one of those posh four-by-fours, Japanese, German, Yankee, whatever."

"Two fellahs getting out, and bless me, dressed in suits with fancy ties. It won't be Health and Safety then. Perhaps it's bankers striking out, scoutin' for new customers, gotta be desperate coming way out here."

"Best we go over and greet 'em afore they start wandering, getting mud over their city shoes. Find out what they be wantin'. Maybe milk marketing folk come to reduce our milk yield money. But rare to do it in person, hah!" He pats Charlotte's side as he readies to stand up.

"On the other hand, perhaps they come to tell us we getting an increase?" grins Mildred, holding out a helping hand.

Tobias, grunting, slowly straightens up. "Living in fairy-tale land if you think that, woman. Anyway it's near enough mid-mornin' break time, a mug of scrumpy sounds attractive. Let's go on over," says Tobias.

"Agreed, husband."

They half-stretch their wellington-clad feet over the straw-strewn floor, exit the barn, leaving Charlotte happily chewing cud, dipping, shaking her head and swishing her tail. Their two black and white border collies yelp and do a merry dance at the appearance of their masters. Barking, bounding, circling the pair as the two trudge, side-by-side along a stone pathway, passing an old John Deer tractor, a rusty, horse-drawn hay rake and several piles of sawn timber. Mr and Mrs ponder on who the newcomers, now standing at the cottage door, could be. Tobias nods towards the vehicle, "Yet another fellah in the back of their motor, like he's trying to keep out of sight, low down, slumped, barely see his head."

Mildred says, "Tall fellah looks businesslike, dashing even. Shorty looks Oriental, dressed gaudy, and just look at all that fluffy hair... oooh! My guess he's Chinese?"

"Can't say, maybe Japanese?" says Tobias.

The strangers look round on hearing the dogs yelping, and the squelch of wellington boots.

"Well, what you fellahs wantin'?" booms Tobias, coming up, stomping on the stone flags, then scraping the cloying mud from his soles and heels on a metal boot scraper set in the ground. He orders the dogs to be quiet, "Down, stay, Ben! Down, stay, Bill!" The dogs obey, sit back on their haunches, panting, tongues lolling, keenly eyeing the two strangers at the door.

The tall man squints in the sunlight, shading his eyes. "Good morning. We're pleased to meet you," he holds out a hand. One of the dogs snarls.

Tobias eyes the hand, doesn't shake it. "We'll see 'bout that. Quiet Ben!"

"I'm Jack Martin, and my colleague here is Mr Ito, Fuzzy Ito," he inclines his head at the little Oriental man: copious black hair, gold ear studs, wearing a tan suit, a blue-yellow tie tucked into a gold waistcoat, brown shoes and clutching a laptop computer under his right arm.

Ito grins, says, "Gleetings," to the Peabody's.

"Ah, Chinese," observes Tobias.

"No. Yapanese," barks Fuzzy, thrusting his chest out. "Best special 'fecks man in UK movie business."

"You come to the right place Mr Ito, we got plenty of special effects hereabouts. Wind-felled trees, some eighty-five acres set with spring oats, all mud and puddles, cows a-calvin', pig and horse shit spread all over, an' five miles of overgrown hedgerow. Still, you didn't come way out here to study country life, eh? Lessen of course, you come to give us a hand?" Tobias angles his head and winks.

"Mr and Mrs Peabody, isn't it?" inquires Jack, smiling at Tobias' quick-fire, if sarcastic, response.

"Yep. So what's this calling on us during our mid-mornin' break, Mr Jack Martin?"

"We were sent in your direction by the landlord at the Shoulder of Mutton in Loughton village," says Jack, casually pushing his hand through his hair.

"Balmy Blair, eh? Sounds 'bout right, knows everyone who knows everything goin' on hereabouts, most of it be tittle-tattle so don't you get to rely on it. What's he been sayin' concerning me and my good lady, to be bringing you all the way out here?" asks Tobias.

"It is not what you think, Mr. Peabody. We're not selling anything, nor are we to do with agriculture. In short, I want to shoot your herd of highland cattle."

"My, my. You behind the times some. Haven't shot cattle hereabouts for some fifty years. Still and all, I guess things be a-changing these modern times. But it sounds like you been misled some." Tobias grins.

"I'm sorry," murmurs Jack, shaking his head in dismay. "I have misled you. I mean, we want to film them. We're from a company called G.E.M.Pix based in Craxton. We are specialists in graphics and special effects for the movie and television industry. We've come here to arrange with you to shoot, er, film, a cattle scene. I'm the manager in charge, Special Effects Manager actually."

"What's all this got to do with us in partic'lar?" asks Mildred.

"We've been making inquiries, searching all round the south west for a herd of highland cattle."

Tobias raises an eyebrow. "Plenty of 'em in Scotland, of that I'm bloody sure."

"But only one herd, in Wiltshire, yours, at least according to the Highland Cattle Association, and those kind folk back at the pub." Jack winces as one of the collies licks his hand in a show of friendship.

"True. Only pedigree highland herd hereabouts. So what?" Tobias demands, thrusting out his jaw.

"We need to film highland cattle for a scene in a movie that is being made here. It is a big budget, action-packed movie. Nothing more sinister than that. To be frank, because we're partly funded by government we're obliged to film local people, scenes, and architecture as much as we possibly can. As well, we're also on a deadline to finish a particular set of scenes before the end of the month. We will, of course, pay a fair price for your time and use of your, er, herd and facilities." Jack flip-flops his wet fingers against his trousers trying to dry them.

This all seems weird to Tobias. Three strangers behaving shifty, two putting themselves out and about with a third crouched in the back of the four-by-four, face puckered up. Yet here they are, out of the blue, offering money to take pictures of his herd of highland cattle. Mind, it is a prize herd, well the bull is. Is this too good to be true? But since it is the twentieth day of the month, could be an early pay-day? First of all these strangers have to be checked-out. He says, "We fresh out of geese layin' golden eggs 'round these parts and we're too long in the tooth… "

Mildred interrupts, smiling wide, "Best y'all come inside. Just saying to Tobias its time for a break, so a pint of cider, home-baked bread, pork pie, cheese, pickle?" her eyes fix on Tobias. "Is that not so husband?"

"Yep. Why'nt you come inside," Tobias unlatches the door and swings it open, toes and heels his wellingtons off, saying, "Better bring yon fellah in from that vehicle of yours. Sunny it may be, but a chill creeps into the bones lessen you be active, on the move," says Tobias.

"Our man in the S.U.V? That's Mr Charles Wren. He is somewhat overwrought. He gets disoriented in these narrow Devon roads, they're like death-traps he says." Jack shrugs, nonchalant.

"Yep. Can be that. What's he here for anyhow?" questions Tobias.

"He's actually one of our bean counters, who likes his comforts, and his scotch."

"Bean counter?" Mildred queries, raises her eyebrows at this odd terminology.

"A money-man. We'll call him in if need be. Look here, Mr Peabody, we did call your number from the Shoulder of Mutton this morning, nobody picked up? We didn't want to come calling unannounced."

"Most of the time we don't hear the telephone ringin'. We're out preparing for milking by half-five, then feedin' the livestock."

"Sorry we missed you."

Tobias shrugs, leads the way, knuckle-pushing an inner door open for Jack to hold. Two old black cats scurry out hissing, the dogs yap and growl at them. They file behind Tobias, into a large, low raftered kitchen dominated by an iron stove. Pots, pans, two dead rabbits, drying out, hang on hooks from an oak-crossbeam, a huge oak dresser taking up almost one wall; on it at one end sits an old-fashioned black telephone, at the other a silver trophy cup with an engraved shield under-written with the words, 'Champion Highland Bull'. Two rocking chairs with crumpled cushions are located either side of the inglenook, and occupying the centre of the kitchen is a long oak dining table, on each side are two wooden benches.

"Do you go to the movies, Mr Peabody?" asks Jack as, invited, they sidle along benches either side of the table, having a wood cutting board, bread saw, condiments, carving knife and a stack of dishes lying on it.

"Got to say yes, on occasion, on holiday. Last time was down in Torquay, two years since." Tobias says.

"What you go see?" barks Ito.

"Can't fully remember," mutters Tobias, "All about monsters, flying creatures and such-like, on an island someplace. Daft fillum I thought."

"Ah, Jurassic Park perhaps?"

"Coulda been," says Tobias, reaching down to grip and hoist a stoneware flagon onto the bench. *Clomp.*

"Many of the prehistoric creatures in that movie were created by people such as ourselves," Jack explains, "using computers." Keep it simple for these country folk.

Geriatricks 1

Ito inches along one bench, his short legs swinging clear of the stone floor. He lays his laptop carefully on the table's rough surface. He smiles, "Iss valable. Velly important piece of kit."

Mildred produces a large wedge of cheese and a jar of pickle while Tobias carefully fills four tankards with cider from the flagon, saying, "Best home-made scrumpy this side of Swindon, to be sure. Got to specially recommend it to you, Fishy, comin' from afar, out East like."

"Is Fuzzy, not Fishy," barks Ito, taking the tankard in both hands. He sips, "Not like sake."

Jack also takes a gulp, forces a grin, rolls his eyes, "G-r-e-a-t taste Mr Peabody."

"You call me Tobias," grants Tobias. Sitting down he quaffs a couple of mouthfuls of cider himself.

"You actually pay for taking pictures of cattle?" inquires Mildred as she saws a crusty home-baked loaf into half-inch thick slices, lays them out on the now put-out dishes. "Pickle, cheese, slice o' pork pie?"

The two nod warily, "We certainly do, Mrs Peabody. We pay our way."

"What pay?" she asks, looking up.

"Depends on how accessible the subject is. We assess time and money."

"Ah, that's why the bean-counter, eh?" says Tobias as he reaches for the carving knife and lays the blade across the slab of cheese. He slams his palm down to create a one-inch chunk. He repeats this four times.

"You're very perceptive, Tobias," says Jack, eyeing the blade.

Tobias' Cattle

"We got our ways," says Tobias, putting the knife down.

"So, to the point," starts Jack, "We have need to film a herd of highland cattle, stampeding." He pauses to nibble on a quarter-slice of pork pie, presented to him by Mildred on a plate, no knife, no fork.

"Can't go upsettin' purebred highland cattle Mr Jack. No way we can do stampedin'," says Tobias, biting on a cheese strip dipped in the pickle jar.

"We merely want them to, er, run across a field. Fuzzy will capture the animals on his movie camera then build up the scene on his studio computer using specialized software. He adds dust, sound-effects, music and 'hey presto' we have a full-blooded stampede, with appropriate background and music."

"Danger is, we get 'em too excited, they bolt, smash gates down an' play havoc all over… "

"Don't fret, we won't overdo it, Tobias. Anyway, you'll be there to see that we and they are okay, okay?"

"Okay, Jack Martin. Another?" asks Tobias, pouring more cider uninvited into the visitors' tankards.

"Highland cattle, impressive-looking animals in the flesh, I dare say," says Jack, as he now delicately sips from his refreshed tankard. He eyes the drink, puffs his cheeks. "I've seen them in, er, films, but not live."

"Highland cattle 'stremely good lookin'. Wide set horns, hairy, sturdy legs. Make best beef."

Suddenly Mildred holds up a finger. "Paying what?" she asks. "Makes sense to understand, eh?"

"Agreed, ma'am. Let me call our money-man in." Jack looks for an easy way to leave the bench.

"You need a money-man to figure how much to pay us?" queries Tobias.

"It's his job, and company policy, I can't by-pass our very important Charles Wren."

"Guess we don't understand your city ways too good," says Tobias, shaking his head.

Jack Martin nods, exiting the kitchen, hoping a breath of fresh air will clear his head.

Mildred starts, "Hey up Fritzy, you'm missing out on the cheese and pickle."

Fuzzy says, "Iss Fuzzy, yes? Tanks, but I stay with the scwumpy, kay?"

"You do that. Got all the country goodness you can ask for in that mix," grins Tobias, "An' more."

Jack, at the S.U.V. opens the rear door and shakes Charles Wren into life. "Charles, stir man, we've got to agree on payment for this highland cattle stampede scene."

Now, coming to, more alert, Charles snarls, "Jack Martin, if you've already struck a… "

"No, its down to you, but I will say that they haven't a got clue. This feeble-minded pair of oldies can't tell the difference between a stocking run and a run on the stock-market. They'll take whatever we offer!"

"Okay," grunts Charles, reaching for his attaché case and slithering out of the vehicle. "Lead the way."

Charles, on Jack's heels, gives a curt nod to the two Peabodys as he enters the kitchen. He hitches up his trousers, perches on the end of the bench, the same side as Ito, placing his attaché case on the table while looking left and right. He nods at the offer of a tankard of cider, ignoring several no, no, no hand signals from Jack from behind Tobias' back. "Right, lets not waste time. Where are we in this matter?"

"These good people have kindly agreed, in principle, to let us film their herd of highland cattle. I have said we would pay a reasonable fee for this service. So, over to you, Charles," says Jack, gesturing.

Charles dramatically click-clacks his attaché case's latches, raises the lid, takes out a slim-line calculator and notepad. He says, easing a silver biro from his top pocket, "In these situations we have a pre-arranged sliding scale for the filming of livestock, as opposed to zoo animals and such." Charles looks around.

"Arrr, just like down at our cattle market?" Tobias grins, knowingly.

Charles sips his cider, "We may sometimes allow leeway according to ease of access for filming, but very often that will be a judgement call by those actually on site." He gestures to Jack and Ito.

"The herd's handy enough in our top seventy-five-acre. Open meadow, few hollows, nowt obstructive," says Tobias.

"Good. Well let us cut the crap… " begins Charles, eying the slab of cheese thrust in front of him.

"Crap? Sure, we got loads of that," says a po-faced Tobias.

"Forget it," grunts Wren, "Look. I can offer you ten pound a head for–"

Tobias interrupts, "Afore we get involved, too far along, I gotta check you fellahs bona-fides. Makes sense these days with everyone and his kin roamin' round the country."

"Check us. Why?" queries Charles.

"Can't have you pretendin' to be who you ain't Mr Charles Wren. Here, out of the blue? That be so?"

"Well here's who we are, with our Craxton office number and address," Charles proffers his business card with an ingratiating smile.

Tobias ignores the card, leaving it on the table. He walks over to the dresser on which is placed the old-fashioned black telephone. He picks up the receiver, dials a number, listens, "That you Balmy? Tobias. I got three fellahs a-visiting in my parlour, come from your place this morning they tells me. They go by the names of Jack Martin, Charles Wren and a Frizzy Ito–"

"Iss Fuzzy!" says Fuzzy Ito, hands clasped around his tankard.

"You still there?" inquires Tobias, eyeing Ito. Then, into the mouthpiece, "You had 'em stay overnight. I want to know if they be of good reputation?" Tobias listens, then, "Okay, I owe you one Balmy."

Charles Wren looks quizzically at Tobias, who says, "You check out okay."

"You found out about us from a–?"

"Balmy looked you up afore he took your card this mornin'. Called London, Craxton and 'nother place."

"What other place?" asks Jack.

Tobias looks at Jack, smiles, saying, "Can't say, confidential. So let's get down to it Jack Martin, Charles Wren, Funny Ito. Ten pound a head, eh?" Tobias resettles on the bench next to Mildred.

Tobias' Cattle

"Iss, Fuzzy!" Ito grins wide as he sups, two-handed, from his tankard.

Charles, "We're basing our figures on a herd of some one hundred cattle, which we are led to understand you have on your farm." He takes a tentative bite of cheese. "Agreeable," he says, licking his lips.

"Reckon filmin' pictures of a prize pedigree herd should be nearer a hundred a head," retorts Tobias, "that sounds more realistic, right enough."

"Oh, that is out of the question–" starts Charles.

"G'bye Mr. Wren." says Tobias, rising to his feet. "Why'nt you get yourselves up to them highlands in Scotland, them tartan farmer folk be mighty pleased to get a tenner a head, to be sure."

"Look," Charles gives a deep sigh, "I can go to twelve pounds a head, but that's all."

"Why per head? How 'bout by the day? Reckon that'd be less cost for you. How 'bout two thousand?" Tobias playfully spins the carving knife below his pointed forefinger.

Mildred says, "Oh, Tobias, that would be a big help in keepin' the place running smooth-like. Two–"

"For goodness sake woman, don't be so bloody ridiculous. We shall pay by the head," snaps Charles.

"Hey-up fellah, you see that telephone over there?" growls Tobias, pointing with a bony finger. The dogs growl, sensing tension. "Mildred dearest, take Bill and Ben outside afore they get uppity with our friend here, wantin' to tear him apart."

Charles Wren nods, apprehensive, wary, "Yeees, I see it?"

Geriatricks 1

"Your Jack's gonna need to dial for an ambulance to mop up bloodstains all over yorn head and body if you speak to my lady such like again. You unnerstand?" snarls Tobias.

"Shut-up, Charles," murmurs Jack. "Calm down and apologise to Mrs Peabody."

Charles Wren shakes his head, "I am sorry Mrs Peabody. But really there is no way I can pay by the day. Shooting is likely to take more than a day. It must be per head. Finito!" Charles looks around casually, then he asks, "Erm, a bathroom?"

"You up to speed with your Eyetalian, but a mite slow with your 'rithmatic," Tobias says, rolling his eyes.

"We got a bathroom, course we 'ave. Why you askin'," says Mildred.

"He wants the lavvy." Tobias says, pointing to a side door. "That-a-way fellah. Turn right, go out back." Charles slides off of the bench and quickly leaves the kitchen, clutching a half-bitten chunk of cheese.

"Works his mouth real well, does that bean-counter fellah of yours," observes Tobias. "Likes of him go down a bundle at our Farmers Union meetings."

"Yes, he does go on rather," agrees Jack, drinking cider.

Tobias reaches for the flagon, pours a good measure into Charles Wren's tankard. They sit in silence until Wren reappears, cheese-less. He reseats himself, shakes his head and reaches for his tankard… he sips the smooth nectar. He smiles, sighs, looks round. "So that's settled then. Twelve pounds a head."

"Right, let's get this show on the road." Jack slides along the bench, preparing to stand. "Tally ho!"

"Hold up, Mr Jack Martin, er, hereby hangs somethin' of a tale," says Tobias, looking over at Mildred with an apologetic tilt of his head.

"Yeeess... " mutters Jack. "Hic!" His steadying fingers splayed, ready to rise.

Tobias straightens, spreads his arms, hands palm-up, appealing, "Truth be, we only got twelve of them highland cattle–"

"Twelve?" repeats a startled Jack.

"Twelve!" echoes Charles. "That's not a bloody herd!"

"Twelve," repeats Tobias. "You'n real quick on the uptake."

"Twelve head," sighs Jack. "We can't shoot a stampede scene with a mere twelve cattle. We'll have to reconsider–"

Tobias continues, "Had to sell considerable number to keep the farm above water. Last month we–"

A gleeful Wren interrupts, "Oh, that's too, too, bad. But it really isn't worth our while continuing."

Ito shoves his tankard in Tobias's direction, indicating a refill. "Iss okay, I have powerful special 'ffects programme. I can fix. I give demo–"

"Shut up, Ito," barks Charles. "It's not going to happen. We're leaving." Charles slams down the lid of his attaché case.

"No! Good idea, give us a demo Fuzzy," invites Jack with a sweep of his hand towards Ito's laptop.

Ito sips from his tankard, then opens the laptop lid–

cum-screen, it grows bright, he swings the laptop round while pressing buttons on the keypad. "We have lelephant stampede scene from last movie we shoot. Five lelephants only 'vailable, we make up number to one hunned, also we cleate dusty, African plairee. See," Ito points to his screen. They lean forward, Charles sniffs at an unpleasant odour seemingly coming from close-by Tobias. They peer at an unfolding African prairie scene where dozens of elephants are shown galloping across a sun-baked, dusty plateau in a panic flight, chased by a fleet of safari dune buggies. The dramatic orchestral score builds excitement in the background. "S'easy with latest CGI plogramme," beams Ito, pointing at the screen, then tapping a couple of keys. His gold ear studs flash as he nods his head excitedly at his creation, albeit months old by now.

"That looks, sounds, real good," growls Tobias.

"Agreed," says Jack. "Some time since I viewed that scene. It's more than good, it's totally brilliant."

"Very impressive," agrees Charles reluctantly. Tobias tops up his tankard, nodding for Mildred to bring another flagon of scrumpy from out back. The lady grins, does as she is bid.

"Looks real real, I do say," admires Tobias.

"It will certainly be a challenge for us to film a herd of twelve, then to build up to two hundred," states Jack, keeping an eye on Charles', knowing his ability to down several tots in minute or two.

"How's your fellah make that machine do tricks like that?" asks Tobias.

"Well Fuzzy starts a scene with just a few elephants,"

explains Jack. "He feeds that scene onto his graphics programme, then he doubles up their number, again and again, until he has a huge herd. Hey presto!"

"Hmmm. Best we show you the cattle so you can be sure we got what you lookin' for," says Tobias.

"We're leaving," says Charles. "There can be no deal with only twelve head. Impossible."

"Don't be a-leavin' afore you take a drop more of Devon's finest Charles Wren. Here now," Tobias pours liquid into Wren's now half-empty tankard. "You quaff that, give you health protection, y'hear?"

"If Fuzzy says it is a go technically Charles, then we should carry on as planned," argues Jack.

Charles tries to focus. "Be it on, on, your head Jack, erm, you're in charge?"

"Do you have spare pairs of wellingtons?" inquires Jack, ignoring Wren, looking over at Mildred.

"Oh, aye. Green uns, black uns, kids spotted uns," she replies.

"Any colour will be fine thank you, ma'am."

"You should get your picturin' done today. Weather be holdin' good for six, seven hours yet," says Tobias.

Charles Wren folds down the lid of his attaché case, "We agree twelve pounds a head. That's one hundred and forty four pounds. I will give you cash right after the today's shoot, Mr Peabody."

"No, that not be right. By my reckonin' we due two thousand and four hundred pounds," says Tobias. He ushers Mildred to one side as the visitors get set to rise from their benches.

"I repeat," says Wren, ignoring Tobias's fantasy

figure. I offered twelve pounds a head, for filming twelve cattle, so one-four-four it is."

"What we have here is you making a miscalculation of a sizeable nature," states Tobias.

"Miscalculation? How dare you. We're, we're, dealing in such small numbers… " he turns, almost overbalancing, as he appeals to Jack. "Do we really need to get into an argument over such a paltry sum? A mere hundred and twenty–"

"A hundred and forty-four, I heard it proper," interrupts Mildred.

"Don't be so bloody… " starts Wren. Jack holds up a hand, beckoning Charles into a huddle. They whisper while Ito occupies himself running the elephant scene over again. Dramatic music echoes around the kitchen. The cheese and pickle forgotten.

"We've got to get this scene in the bag," whispers Jack to Charles. "No room for manoeuvre, we're under pressure, and should I remind you that our director is calling us to screen this scene next bloody week, man. I can't willy-nilly allow us to back away from this opportunity. Damn it Charles, we're already on site."

"These country hicks aren't going to hold me to ransom, Jack. So, so, we stay put with my figures."

"No, as field director I say we compromise. There's nowhere else in this part of England where there's a herd of highland cattle. You know it, I know it and God help us, Tobias-bloody-Peabody knows it."

"A herd? That's a frigging joke. Fifteen a, hic, head, and that's final," insists Charles.

Mildred sees Jack and Charles Wren exchange

words behind hands, and Ito seated, eyes sparkling and glued to his screen. She nudges Tobias, "You're pressin' too hard Tobias. Work them a little so as we can be sure of something worthwhile, don't throw away money sittin' on a platter."

"M'dear, I know there ain't another herd of highland cattle this side of the Isle of Wight, Essex Cornwall or otherwise south of the Scottish border. They'll come round. They've need of a drop more scrumpy, then I'll get negotiatin' proper. That Wren fellah's already swivel-eyed," Tobias turns round, opens and rummages about in one of the dresser's drawers.

"That horrible Wren fellah," says Mildred, "he won't come round, an' with you tormentin' him, he'll dig his heels in."

"Fellah like that needs tormentin'. We got him on the run. Wait and see my Mildred."

Jack whispers to Charles, "You told me just last week you had budgeted something like four thousand pounds for this cattle-stampede scene-take."

"That was then. Plus we have to take our travel and living expenses into account. Anyway, this Tobias chap is playing games. I will not have, have, it," slurs Charles.

"A minute ago you said they were country hicks," says Jack.

"Oh, all right. Fifteen tops, okay?"

Jack nods. They look across at Tobias and Mildred engaged in conversation the other side of the kitchen. "Ahem!" Jack harrumphs loudly to trigger a resumption of their discussion. Ito looks up, "Repeat demo?"

"No, that was enough, very impressive," Jack says.

He waves away a proffered refill of his tankard with a deep sigh. The four reseat themselves on the benches together with Ito.

"Heavy rain forecast for tomorrer. Best get your picture-takin' done today," urges Mildred. "Get busy while the sun's a-shinin'. That dependin' on we gettin' the figures set right, right?"

"We have one further offer as a gesture of our goodwill. Then we'll go to work," Jack smiles.

"Fifteen per head," joins Charles Wren. "Thus giving a total of one hundred and eighty pounds."

"No" says Tobias,. "By my reckoning two hundred head at, now you saying fifteen pounds a head, is three grand. Yep! That'll make me and Mildred real happy, not to mention Mr Fawkes down at the bank."

"You can't be serious," says an astonished Charles. He pauses to swallow from a seemingly never-empty tankard. "How on earth do you arrive at that outrageous figure?"

"You better get that calculatin' machine out again. What we got here is a sizeable miscalculation on your part. Trust you're not tryin' to cheat me and my Mildred here."

"Miscalculate! Cheat! How dare you!" states Charles, waving a rubbery arm in the air.

"No problem with the darin', the problem is yorn figures. You picturin' twelve of my highland cattle, then you reckon to somehow make them two hundred strong on Itzy Fritzy's computer machine. They still all be my cattle, whichever way up you looks at it. No twelve highland cattle, no two hundred for your stampedin' picture. Can't be straightforwarder than that?" Tobias grins, angles his head, "So it be three grand."

"It's Fuzzy!" pleads Ito.

"Tobias has a point, Charles," says Jack thoughtfully. "And, we really have to get a move on," he shrugs, inclining a questioning head at Charles, "Still, it's well inside the budget, eh?"

"Perhaps," Charles muses, "we should reconsider a day-rate. You said two thousand, earlier Mr Peabody. I'll settle on that figure for a day and a half, that would be the best for all concerned. Can we agree?"

Jack adds, "Same money, even if it takes a day or two longer, say, due to adverse weather."

"Well, I then be takin' a gamble on you being here perhaps 'nother three, five days further on, waitin' on sunshine while me getting sweet bugger-all if it keeps on a-rainin'. Yes?" observes Tobias.

"Oh?" exclaims Jack, shocked at Tobias slipping into the vernacular. "Urm, well… "

"We got a tradition runnin' hereabouts," purrs Tobias, winking at Mildred, "We toss a copper coin when we need to settle on a close-run thing. Nothing life and death like, but a regular happening when we get to tie-break on occasion. Goes on a lot down at the Shoulder of Mutton – settlin' dart, domino an' shove-ha'penny disputes," Tobias shrugs, "Kinda stops fisticuffs and Balmy's bar gettin' smashed up Saturdays."

"A close-run thing?" utters Charles Wren in astonishment, now fired-up at this turn of event.

"Gotta say difference 'tween two an' three thousand, that be a close-run thing," says Tobias.

"I'll bet it is… to you, Mr Peabody," mutters Charles, casually reaching for his tankard.

"Seems reasonable in the circumstances," agrees Jack, smiling at Tobias's guile and Wren's discomfort. "It would settle matters, Charles, once and for all?" Jack himself finds it difficult to focus.

Ito says, "In Yapan we belief in yamasatzu. Grood thing come from tossing shaved bamboo stick in air."

"Dear God, save me from Eastern philosophical mumbo-jumbo," bleats a watery-eyed Charles Wren.

"Straightforward ain't it?" says Tobias. "You sayin' a day-and-a-half for two thousand, but could be you get into stayin' a coupla days or more if bad weather sets in, kickin' your heels, gettin' under our boots. Yet me wanting three thousand, however long it takes for you to do your filmin'," says Tobias.

Jack eyes Charles, neither can quite get their heads around this country logic. He looks at his wristwatch, "Look, we're losing time. Let us wrap this up and get moving."

Charles moans, head in his hands, "For God's sake. Two verses three thousand pounds, that is hardly a close-run thing, and one hell of a long way from one-eight-zero pounds."

"It's the best way to settle it" argues Jack. "Filming a half day today, and a full day tomorrow if need be, then we're done. We get the better deal if we win the toss – and with your luck, Charles, we surely will?"

"Let me get this straight, Jack," says a bemused, perspiring, Wren. "You want me, your fully qualified accountant, to agree a business deal that will be decided by the flip of a coin? All without Fuzzy yet to point his camera and this, sight unseen, bloody twelve-strong highland so-called herd. That's pure gambling?"

"Choosing twix one thing or t'other, that ain't gamblin'," interrupts Tobias. "That be fair."

"We toss a coin," states Jack, beginning to enjoy this cantankerous old sod's unpredictability. "Otherwise we'll be arguing all afternoon."

"Yon Jack Martin's got a point," says Tobias, "you sit around any longer, you be disruptin' our day too. Can't have my Mildred hollerin' and screamin' about not readying for milkin' as she oughta be!"

"Let's do it," says Jack. "Mission Control… we have lift off!"

"So," says Tobias, "we got three thousand to me and Mildred, you filmin' as long as you want, gainst you payin' two grand an' bein' here for a day and a half, and if'n the weather looks like delayin' you some, that be too bad, you get off my land." Tobias fishes around in his trouser pocket, pulls out a soiled handkerchief and handful of coins and, with a flourish, spews them onto the table. He repockets the handkerchief, selects up a two-penny piece, balancing it on the folded thumb of his right fist, in traditional coin-flipping stance. He looks around. "Ready? My cattle, my call. You okay with that?" mute nods from Charles, a grinning Ito and a stern Jack.

Tobias spins the coin into the air calling, "Heads."

They all watch the spinning, flashing, coin in flight. The coin rises, arcs and clatters down onto the oak table. Tobias says to a bemused Charles Wren, "You best look yourself, see what side we got."

Charles shoves his tankard to one side, leaning forward to peer closely at the coin. He scowls, "Heads."

"Well dang me if it ain't," explodes Tobias, grinning. Jack also looks and nods. "Sure enough, heads"

"Good call eh? If'n I do say so meself," says Tobias, looking over at his grinning wife.

"Ooooh," sighs Mildred. "This will take a money-weight off our back, husband."

"Three thousand. Right, how you gonna pay?" demands Tobias.

"We'll send you a cheque within thirty days," says Charles, struggling to rise from the bench.

"This may be a tiresome situation, an' I know you wanna be gettin' on quick like, but I got me an idea for your consideration. Get you in real good with your financin' people back there in pin-stripe city?"

Charles sighs, unsteady on his legs: "And… what, what, idea is that Mr Peabody?" He sits down again.

"Double or quits come to be a regular thing down at the Shoulder of Mutton… "

Jack looks askance at this suggestion.

Charles says, "You will… let-us-take-our-scene-shots-for-no-payment-if-you-lose?" spells out Charles. Oh, ho, here's his chance to turn the tables on this daft old reprobate. Law of averages, the next toss the coin will fall tails up.

Jack waves both hands in the air at seeing Charles run through the odds in his addled brain. "Look, we have to get on, Charles, leave it at three thousand, yes?"

Tobias watches Wren with eagle eyes. Spur him on some. "You got the makin' of a top casino-player, Mr

Wren. I can't see likes of me comin' close to your sharp 'telligence you demonstratin' here today. It being a real pleasure meeting with you," Tobias pours the coins from one hand to the other, teasing.

Jack looks up, who will outsmart who? Never bloody mind. He needs some fresh air. He nudges Ito to move, they both crouch to start shuffling along the bench.

Tobias readies and steadies the two-penny-piece on a yellow thumbnail. He looks at Charles with an engaging smile. "I'm sure gonna rue the day I came up against a champion bean counter the likes of you, Charles Wren."

Eyes narrowing, Charles nods okay for Tobias to toss the coin. Tobias makes a perfect flip, calling 'heads' as the spinning coin arcs through the air. Five pairs of eyes fix on the flashing coin, supposedly of the realm. Wren clasps his hands together, knuckle-white. Gravity wins, clatter, clatter, then a slow noisy oscitation: whirr, whirr, whirr. The coin flops, flat… silence. The five lean forward, *heads or tails?*

"My, my," smiles Tobias, "Looks like–"

"Yes, yes," chips in a blurry-eyed Charles. "Tails?"

"Wrong Mr Wren, it be heads again," Tobias looks around. No dissent. He sweeps the coin along with others scattered nearby, off the table into his waiting palm and, with a flourish, sends them clattering into the open dresser drawer. "Settled then," says Tobias. "Six grand. You stay a fortnight if'n you so need," he circles Mildred's waist with a strong arm, purses his lips and kisses her on her brow. "There missus, we now got a penny or two to get us along to Southend after gettin' the harvest in. Yeah!"

"How's 'bout cash, saving all that post business?" asks Mildred, smiling broadly at Charles.

"S,s,sorry, Mrs Peabody," stutters a downcast Wren. "We don't carry cash in those amounts with us."

"Well, so you don't forget where we're at, here's a post with our address written on it." Mildred takes out an old crumpled envelope from the still-open dresser drawer, passes it to Charles, who opens his attaché case, drops it in then slaps the lid down.

"Okay, go, go, go," urges Jack Martin. "Fuzzy, you ready?"

"Me good and leddy," beams a glassy-eyed Ito, folding up his laptop. "I go change into film gear in back of SUV. Gimme a few minni, eh?"

Charles Wren refastens his attaché case with a 'snap-snap'. Then, hand outstretched to help to stand, he grasps his attaché case and moves unsteadily toward the door, shaking his head.

"You want to pictures of our prize highland bull, Jack Martin? He be nearby, a paddock in the yard, not up at the meadow. A right cantankerous sod he is. No charge." Tobias chuckles, his cheeks aglow.

"We'll pass on your prize bull for now," says Jack, getting off of the bench. "I think we've enough on our hands with the cattle up in the field." He adds, with grudging admiration, "Tobias, well done this morning."

"We moonrakers get to be fortunate once in a while," says Tobias, with a wink.

"Moonrakers?" queries Jack.

"Wiltshire natives be moonrakers, y'see."

"No I don't," says Jack.

"Another time Mr Jack Martin, another time."

"Tell me, isn't there anybody else to help with work on the farm?"

"Yep. One bachelor son, Jonathan, one married son, David, daughter-in-law's Gillian and three action-packed grandkiddies." Tobias chuckles. "Know each of 'em by name too."

"I'm sure you do," murmers Jack, creaking on straightening up.

"Thas a big family, where they all live?" asks Ito, looking for a way out.

"Here and there," says Tobias. And with a sweep of his arm, "That-a-way Fritzy," he points the way out.

"Iss Fuzzy, Fuzzy, Fuzzy," intones Ito wearily, laptop clutched to his chest.

"Now, best you give me some time while I be putting the Bill and Ben in the pick up, then you follow me along a stone track to the seventy-five-acre. Don't you be a worryin' none, your four-by-four'll cope okay."

"Why the dogs?" asks Jack.

"Need 'em to spook the cattle, get 'em to create a serious gallop for your picture-makin'," says Tobias.

"Wellies just inside the door," advises Mildred. "You'll see 'em."

"Thank you for, for the refreshments," says Jack.

"You be welcome," says Tobias. "An' don't worry 'bout drivin' over my land if you're a mite tipsy. Our Constable Wells be at the Shoulder o' Mutton this time o' day. I do reckon you'll be ready to blow into his tube successful like by the time you get back to the highway, after your filmin' work's done, should he be out patrolling on his bike."

Jack and Charles slowly take their shoes off, struggle to pull on bulky wellingtons, while Ito disappears into the rear of the SUV to change. Wellie-clad, the two clump outside into shimmering sunny daylight and plod over to the SUV, lift the rear door to check Ito has changed and is ready with the filming equipment.

"Rokay," Ito mutters, still yet struggling to put on his working clothes in the confines of the vehicle.

Then, grumbling to each other, Jack and Charles wearily climb into the vehicle and slump down, waiting for Tobias to appear to lead the way to the so-called seventy-five-acre meadow.

Tobias pushes the cottage door to, turning to Mildred. Their eyes meet. She wrinkles her nose at him. He says, "I couldn't have planned it better if'n the Oracle himself was a-working today's action."

"Real nervous that Wren fellah. Makes my flesh creep. I thought he was goin' to... " Mildred starts.

"Wonder-boy's too addicted to money-ways and booze. The devil's got him by the coat tails."

"You a devil yourself, husband. Bless me, that double-headed two-penny-piece trick?"

"Hush woman, they may be lackin something up top, but that don't necessary go for their hearin'."

Tobias opens his arms wide, Mildred moves in, they hug, chuckle, circle and dance a merry jig.

***

Tobias Peabody clumps into the kitchen in stocking feet. "Bless me, Charlotte's calf's doing real well, standin', wobbly, sucklin' and… "

"Postie's been Tobias," interrupts Mildred. "A smart-looking letter with a fancy picture on it, G.E.M.Pix. That's them filming fellahs that was here, right?"

"Yep. About time too. Four weeks since they came a-filming. Heard narry a thing from 'em since."

"Open it," says Mildred, as she lifts the lid off a huge pot on the iron hob to ladle steaming vegetable soup into two bowls. "It'll be our payment."

"Looks like it," says Tobias, tearing the envelope open with a crude thumb. He tugs out a letter, and a cheque. "Yep, reckon this be it."

"We could do with funding next month's hay-making labour and a bit over for a holiday break. I don't want us to face that Mr Fawkes down at the bank again, asking for more money," moans Mildred.

Tobias sits down, hooks on his reading glasses, squinting at the cheque. "Well bugger me!"

"Oh, what it is husband?" Mildred comes over, places a hand on Tobias' shoulder.

"S'cuse me swearing' Mildred, but numbers on this cheque read one hundred and eighty pounds."

"Well that can't be right. I remember we got to agree six thousand?"

"As you say wife. Six grand it was."

"Perhaps Tobias, it's part payment? Or, heaven forbid, they haven't got six thousand."

"Look woman, they're a proper big company, they got plenty money for the likes of taking pictures, an' makin' them special effects and such. Like that Fishy Ito fellah showed us on his machine."

"What's the letter say?" she asks.

"Wait on. Pour me a tankard of cider Mildred," asks Tobias, as he reads the letter. "It says, for filming highland cattle scene at fifteen pounds per head. Please find a cheque enclosed to the value of one hun'ard and eighty pound. Letter's signed by that Mr Charles Wren. He's friggin' gone and diddled us, he's using' figures he said about afore we tossed the coin twice over and agreed six thousand pounds."

"That ain't right, Tobias. You get on that telephone," She points to the black telephone on the dresser, "You get it put right."

"Doubt that be enough to shift his sort Mildred, for sure I'm not sittin' here and phonin' day-by-day. Me and the boys will work out some direct action to secure our money. Proper amount. Tell me woman, where you put that flash business card that Wren fellah gave us?" he asks.

"In the dresser drawer, 'long with that dud two-penny-piece of yours," she grins.

Tobias stands up, pulls the dresser drawer open, rummages, takes out Charles Wren's business card and looks at it. "Yep. They got head office along Craxton High Street. I reckon that's our best move, we go and meet them in person, persuade them to do the right thing."

"Oh, Tobias. We don't want no trouble, like fightin'. You already in Constable Wells' notebook."

"I take account of what you say my dearest. Yep, I ain't no brain-match to confront them lawyer-types they employ to fight their corner. No, I gotta think this through," he sips his cider thoughtfully. "Ah, ha, I know a way we can influence a change of mind in them, what Jack Martin calls, bean counters. Well them bean counters are going to find it unwise to break a promise with us Peabodys. We are going to give them their cumuppance first hand Mildred, first hand. Now, I got to go chat to Jonathan and David. They'll help figure what best to do. Granted I'll probably get 'em seeing my way of thinking," growls Tobias.

"Finish your soup," says Mildred. "Keep your strength up."

* * *

"Jonathan, I'll pick up David from his cottage, you go collect his lady to go help load five of them highland cattle in the wagon, all steady like. I 'specially want that Dorothy along, she got an arse like a blow-torch, just what I need to do some persuadin', then you meet me here. Meantime I'm loadin a couple of hundredweight of cake for their feeding," he chuckles, saying, "They're goin' to be hungry travelling all the way to Craxton. I'll lead the way. I got a town map ready showing where we got to go."

"Yes, Pa,"

"Now remember son, soft-pedal in town. They seeing you hot-roddin' along the high street in a cattle wagon and you could get apprehended like before, and

I don't want our license plate being written up twice over in their record office. Yet again, no delayin' on this day in particular. Goddit?"

"Yes, Pa."

Tobias smiles as his youngest son trundles out of the farmyard driving the farm's cattle wagon. He waves a brief salute as he steps back into the cottage doorway. "We're off now, Mildred," he bellows. "You keep them dogs in here while we move off. Did you ready-pack cheese sandwiches, pickle, a flask o' cider and a couple of mugs for the lads?"

"Hush yourself husband, I ain't deaf. Here." Mildred hurries forward, hands him a bulky hessian bag. "Now are you sure you got the right timing to do this whatever thing?"

"Wednesday, mid-mornin', just about right enough I reckon."

"Don't get into trouble Tobias, no upsettin' the law. You hear me?" Mildred stuffs another two wrapped packages into the canvas bag. She goes back for the flask of cider and places it in the bag as well.

"Yeah woman, I hear you. Look out for us 'round late afternoon, be back for milkin' and muckin' out."

"Mutton stew, potatoes, onions, swedes and carrots for you then," Mildred says.

"Don't forget to be warmin' up that apple pie I smell a-baking." Tobias runs his tongue over his lips.

Mildred walks over, reaches out, places her hands each side of his face, stretches up and kisses him full on the lips.

"Wasn't expectin that. Phew!" he puffs, smiling broadly.

"Good luck husband as you go galivantin' about town? I'm repeatin', be careful of them town coppers."

He chuckles as he ambles out of the cottage, over to his ancient Land Rover. He unlatches the driver's door, swings the canvas bag onto the middle seat, sits himself down, starts the engine and rumbles over tractor-made ruts to the feed barn. He turns round, backs up, opens up, and hefts four bags of feed into the back of the pick up. He motors a few feet, stops, gets out, closes the barn door, reseats himself and leans back to await the boys' return, since they'll be coming through the farmyard on their way to Craxton.

"Weather's good, sunny and warm, just right for the little action we hellfirin' Peabodys got in mind for you graspin', bean countin', cheatin' Charlies," he murmurs, smiling.

* * *

They are motoring steadily along Craxton High Street. David, seated in the Land Rover, with Tobias driving, peers around, he points, saying, "That's it, Pa, that big dark glass building, in the town square, near enough opposite the Town Hall. Can't see any place to park though."

"Yep, I see it," replies Tobias, ducking his head to get the sun out of his eyes. "Jonathan behind us?"

David swivels his head. "Yep, Pa. Following close."

Tobias indicates right and steers the Land Rover ready to cross the stream of oncoming traffic, he waits for a break in the dozens of vehicles coming towards them. Then, foot pressuring the accelerator, he pulls in front of a hesitant-moving red mail van, stopping the traffic flow. Horns blare, a giant fist appears and is shaken furiously out of the van driver's window. Tobias gives him a grin and the finger as he passes in front of Mr Big Fist. He mounts the pavement, brakes to allow a half dozen pedestrians to scuttle past the front of his bumper. Then he carefully motors between two bollards onto a cobbled area surrounding a decorative fountain in the centre of the plaza, off the town square. Tobias inches forward, looking for an entrance in the glazed exterior of the multi-storey building. He espies it when he sees two people coming out. He stops, he says, "David, go direct Jonathan to a spot somewhere between me and that door, while watching out for those daft bollards. Turn him round and get the back end of the cattle wagon real close up."

"Afore I do that Pa, you got in mind gettin' those cattle circling' in front of this place, right?"

"No David, then the folk inside only get to see 'em through those shiny windows, call the police and such like. No, I'm goin' to herd them cattle into their posh domain, then they get first hand special effects," he chuckles. "I do believe they got those security cameras devices set up inside the place. Making for action pictures for the local tele news, when the shit hits–"

"Pa! Ma says you ain't to use bad – hold hard, our beasts got horns wide as a truck, how we gonna herd 'em through that narrow doorway?" David queries.

"You're not observin' proper David. Look a them folk coming and going, see?" Tobias points.

"Ah, yeah, they got those double automatic doors. I see a couple of folk side-by-side walking in. Fair enough, Pa. Let's get moving?" David slides out of his seat.

Tobias watches in his rear-view mirror the cattle truck belching exhaust fumes as it mounts and sways over the pavement's kerb. Jonathan, obeying David's beckoning hand signal, rounding near ninety degrees to draw in close behind the pick up. Tobias stops the engine, places his open town map to one side and steps out. He stands tall, hitches his trouser-belt and surveys the scene around him. "Ah, I reckon I got it near enough about right," he murmurs.

He turns, watches David motioning Jonathan to reverse the truck even closer to the building's doorway. Tobias steps in to take control of the last manoeuvre, saying, "back-up... back-up... back-up". Satisfied, he makes a slice gesture across his throat, Jonathan kills the truck's engine. Inside the rear of the truck the cattle are restless, pawing the straw-strewn deck, bellowing, snorting, barging against the slatted wood-sided panels. They are frightened, thirsty, hungry and want to be released from their confinement.

Tobias motions Jonathan and David to wait apiece. He hefts a sack of feed from the Land Rover across his broad shoulders and strides into the building, doors automatically sliding apart as he breaks the beam. Inside the sunrise-designed blue and pink carpeted atrium there is an atmosphere of peace and calm with movie theme music burbling in the background. Dominant all round are wall-hangings depicting dramatic and famous

Geriatricks 1

film scenes. Central in the atrium is a modern S-shaped chrome reception desk. Sat behind it with a telephone to her ear, is a pretty, bob-tailed brunette wearing a cerise top with a fluffy decorative scarf spun artistically round her neck. Ever alert, she eyes Tobias with suspicion. Here is a man, outside the norm: wellington boots, corded trousers, leather jerkin, open-necked shirt with rolled-up sleeves, tanned, sinewy, veined arms, steel-grey eyes, matching hair, belligerent stance, wearing a grim smile, with a huge hessian sack slung across his shoulder, all conveying to the young lady here is a person with a mission. Those visiting G.E.M.Pix's town offices are usually smart, suited, attaché case equipped, business oriented film producers and directors. Actors, film crews and weirdos are directed to their out-of-town studios. So possibly this fellow is a crazy actor trying to find the company's out-of-town studios.

She stands up to confront the man – just as Tobias dumps the huge sack right on top of the ornate desk with a scrunch. "Bugger me lass, if these feed-sacks don't get a darned sight heavier by the day."

"Sir, how may I be of help?" she asks as sternly as she can.

"I be here to collect some money from Mr Charles Wren. P'raps you tell him Tobias Peabody is stood here wanting to be recompensed for services to… " Tobias reads the sign behind the desk, "… G.E.M.Pix."

"Is Mr Wren expecting you sir? Do you have an appointment?" she asks.

"No young lady. That would be unwise knowing his kind of person."

"Well, I really don't-"

"Get on yon phone, get him down here with his cheque-book, quick-like. You hear me?" Tobias growls.

"I'll call his secretary. Please sir, do sit down won't you?"

"No lass, I'm not a-sittin' down, but I can wait a few minutes while you round him up."

The girl raises an eyebrow as she punches numbers on her phone console. "Belinda I, erm, have a Mr Tobias Peabody here to speak to Mr Wren. There seems to be a problem with a payment. Would you be a pal and get Mr Wren to come down and sort it out?" she dangles the receiver from delicate fingers and appraises Tobias while she waits for a response from Belinda. Time drags. Then a tinny voice, she listens, grimaces, places the receiver on its rest. She says, "Mr Wren is in an important budget meeting and won't be able to see you today. However his secretary asks if you would care to make an appointment-"

"No lass. You didn't convey my meanin' proper. I came here to collect monies due to me, not make an appointment for some days or weeks to come. Unnerstand?"

"Sir, I am not in a position to do anything other than-"

"Maybe lass. But I am," Tobias stands back, looks about the atrium with mock interest. "Best I get on with my deliverin."

"You have a delivery?" she asks.

"Yes lass. For filmin' – kind of."

"You're in the movie business?" soothing talk, get him on side.

"True to say we got some minor experience, viewin' special effects," Tobias says, with a crooked smile.

"You should have said. I will explain how to find our out-of-town studios. You will find a Mr Jack Martin there, he's one of our scene directors. He will–"

"Sorry lass, you getting caught up in somethin not of your makin'. Already met Jack Martin. Today I'm here to meet Charles Wren, your money man and, I say, inside of ten minute, latest."

"And I said that he is otherwise–"

"You got a name, miss?"

"Janet Morgan," She fingers her name badge attached to a cord round her neck.

"Why'n't you call Charles Wren one more time Miss Janet? To be sure he understands what's goin' on down here. Persuade him to come visit me?

"I don't comprehend what you mean, Mr Peabody," the girl says, on the defensive.

"Look about Miss Janet, this a great location for special effect filmin'. But I reckon this fine carpet will look pretty tatty after my cattle get finished millin', bellowin' and shittin' all over it. Got a cattle truck outside, and my boys are waitin' on me to signal them to unload our pedigree herd of highland cattle."

Janet, eyes wide, once again presses the keys to speak to Belinda, "Belinda the situation is becoming a little urgent here in reception. I really do want Mr Wren to get involved. Mr Peabody would seem to be here to, well, take part in a special effects scene of some sort. He insists, demands, to speak to Mr Wren personally... if you would, it would take the sting out of... oh thank you." She looks up at Tobias saying, "We're trying to get Mr Wren to break away from his meeting and speak to you personally."

Tobias smiles wide. "You want to be calling Jack Martin while you busy with the phone, you tell him to hot-foot it along here from out of town. He'll be real upset missing a chance to capture a special effects picture... you got that." He hefts the sack of feed off the counter and onto his shoulder. He walks in a wide circle of the carpeted atrium, comes up to an array of soft-cushioned armchairs spaced round a fine glass-topped designer-table, dumping the sack on the table.

Janet prods the mobile numbers to get Jack Martin, she needs to confirm this scary man has the right to be making a scene here at HQ. Jack responds. She explains the situation to an alert, albeit puzzled Jack Martin. Then, to her horror, she sees Tobias knife-slitting the dumped sack. Then he grabs it to his chest and walks around the atrium shaking out the contents in rows. That done he throws the empty sack on the table, sits in one of the armchairs, pats its arms in mock admiration, lays back and stretches his legs. Janet slowly replaces the receiver leaving Jack speaking into the ether. With tremulous authority, she yells, "Mr Peabody, you just can't go spoiling our carpet like that. You just–"

"Sure you go ahead an' protest, Miss. But spoilin'? Nah, that's just a sprinklin' o' cattle feed, you can get your cleanin' people to sweep it up in a jiffy, providin' that Wren fellah appears in the next few minutes."

She should call Stephen in security. Yes, definitely, but not without giving due consideration to–

Tobias stands up and ambles over to the receptionist's desk. "Janet, tell me, he comin' down to see me with my payment?"

"Do be patient and relax, Mr Peabody," she flutters her eyelashes, appealing to his masculine decency. Then... a small thrill wanders up her spine. He is actually very handsome, in a savage sort of way.

"I'm relaxed enough lass. Doubt if that Mr Wren of yours is going to be though," says Tobias.

"I called Mr Martin to let him know you're here for a, er, scene-shoot." Pacify him somehow, for God's sake. She sits down and is about to punch the keys to get security involved when a buzz, buzz on the console overtakes her intention. Janet puts the receiver to her ear, listens – holds up a free hand creating an 'okay' sign with thumb and forefinger to Tobias, then turns her back to him. He admires her bobbing bob-tail and slender neck as she relates events into the mouthpiece while waving an animated hand.

Meanwhile, assorted people continue walking in and out of the atrium area, passing the desk, heading to and from the elevator, giving little mind to the rows of corn-feed spread around the carpeted floor.

Another couple of bobs. Janet turns, mouthing 'wait-a-minute', lays the receiver down and rises to her feet to walk around the end of the counter. After a stretch-skirt stalk to the front of the glazed frontage to cast a searching look outside, she returns to speak affirmatively into the mouthpiece, then she passes the receiver over the counter to Tobias:, "Mr Peabody, its Mr Wren to speak to you."

"Yep," Tobias barks. He listens. Then, "Seems we didn't get that filmin' done proper that day you come to our farm with Jack Martin and Frosty Ito. Got me to thinking that's maybe why you didn't pay the full amount due to Mildred and me. My lady's real upset we somehow musta done less than you asked of us. So minding to put matters right, I says to her, 'I'll take my boys with five o' them highland cattle direct to that Mr Wren to get the job finished proper, so we can get paid as agreed. Mr Wren, him being a clever fellah, shuffling company figures around all day long with his adding machines, he will be understandin' our situation'. So here we are, Charles Wren, cattle ready for filmin' – or payin' for, or both."

Tobias listens in, "No, we already here as yon pretty Janet just told you. Five, six minutes and pedigree cattle will be millin' round your fine establishment. Lessen, of course, you want to postpone the action by giving over our dues. I'm mindful, since we done all this travellin' and whatever, to be chargin' you a mite more… " Tobias listens, then he says, "Well if you can't be accommodatin' me, I'll be signalling the boys to unload our pedigree cattle," adding, "You be a real stubborn fellah I do say. Just now I asked Miss Janet here to call your Jack Martin to get with that Fuddy Ito fellah and come along over here with his cameras 'cause we be creating some special, special effects! Now, you minded to cough up some money?" Tobias grimaces into the mouthpiece, "Well, what you say in your picturin' parlance? 'Get them cameras rollin' hey-ho and a bloody nonny no!'"

Handing the receiver back to the receptionist Tobias says, "I reckon Miss, you best be bracing yourself for visitors the like you never seen afore and won't be seein' again! Suggest you take shelter, maybe you go someplace upstairs," he raises his eyes to the balconies rising in ranks above their heads. "And, maybe as well you should be calling your cleanin' people to get ready with a hosepipe wi' a couple o' yard brooms. They gonna be needing 'em soon enough."

"Why, what are you going to do?" queries Janet, eyes widening in anticipation of trouble ahead.

"I suffered something of a setback with Mr Charles Wren, Miss Janet. So we now be preparin' for them highland cattle to be creating a scene right here," he nods toward the entrance. "They being a long-horn cattle, irate and getting real aggressive about now, I do suggest you go find someplace safe," Tobias says.

"I repeat Mr Peabody, What are you going to do?"

"Unloadin' cattle, that's what!"

"I will call security if you're going to be–"

Tobias strides toward the entrance, waving at his boys as he passes through the sliding doors.

Janet, grimaces and urgently presses buttons on her console.

Tobias, outside, calls to watchman David, "Any sign of police, traffic warden folk?"

"No, Pa. But we got a small crowd gatherin'," he nods to a knot of people standing by, onlooking.

Tobias' Cattle

Tobias to Jonathan, "I want two beasts coming into the building for now. One to be Dorothy. Yep?"

"Okay Pa, got it," Jonathan swings open the two upper doors, then lowers the ramp of the cattle truck to the ground, hand-hauls two palings to one side. Using a long stick, he prods three animals to the front of the interior separating them from the other two. David assists in placing two hurdles on the ground to prevent the cattle running loose, to guide them towards the building's doorway.

"Okay Pa, ready up?" says Jonathan.

"Yep son,' Tobias bellows, "send 'em on down."

Whack! Whack! Inside the truck Jonathan persuades the two animals to venture out. Then, snorting and shaking their heads, they clatter down the wooden ramp and into the funnel-shaped area. They come to a standstill, trembling, puzzled, eyes wide, flashing. Tobias lifts aside a hurdle and steps into the area and walks up to the two animals, he strokes and pats their hindquarters to quieten them. He walks into the building's door beam – they glide smoothly apart.

"Okay, lets be goin' Jonathan," he yells. Thwack, thwack! The two animals leap forward, Tobias beside them, and burst into the reception area, the atrium. Janet leaps to her feet, her haughty demeanour completely evaporating. She yells, "Security! Security! Here, now, now, now!" she rapidly hoists her backside onto the desk's shiny surface, swinging her shapely legs up and over. She starts to tremble at the sight of these two huge, monsterous, out-of-this-world, creatures.

* * *

The cattle, drooling spittle, horned-heads swinging left and right, gallop straight over to the reception desk. At random, here and there, the animals nose about, snort, sniff, snort, sniff. Curious. *Food?* They move to the heaps of cattle-feed Tobias earlier spewed on the floor in the armchair area. Slurp, gobble, slurp. For a moment they are quiet and content, tails swishing.

Tobias moves across to Janet perched on top the reception desk, knees tucked tight under chin, arms wrapped round her all-of-a-quiver pretty legs. Her silver, stiletto-heeled shoes, one awry, the other laying discarded on the floor. He places an elbow nonchalant on the counter. "D'you reckon you are safe enough up there?" he asks with a smile. He places a comforting hand on her back, patting her gently.

"Get them animals out of here," she cries. "I've called security and the police. Get them out of here."

"All in good time, lass. I've got business to conclude with your bean counter, Charles Wren."

Just then Dorothy's tail straightens out and loops the loop, a loud ripping, tearing, squelching sound reverberates around the atrium as the animal defecates a near-horizontal stream of fecal steamy, brown liquid molasses, which spews and splashes all over the blue and pink carpet. Splosh, splash, splosh.

"Oooh my God. You're in a lot of trouble, Mr Peacock," Janet shouts, a pink hanky covering her nose.

Tobias, "Sounds like a brass band playin' end piece to that Ravel chap's Bolero. Don't it just?"

Tails swishing, the animals continue munching their feed. Dorothy's mate paws the carpet with a hoof – then she too defecates with considerable force.

"Not exactly fragrant, is it?" Tobias observes, gripping the edge of the counter with both hands, looking across at the animals. "Dung stinks, alway has. Never mind lass, comes a time when stirring things up be necessary to get things moving in the right direction."

As Tobias looks at the animals crunching their feed he observes a blue-uniformed security man warily approaching the two highland cattle. The man takes out and speaks urgently into his mobile phone, glaring daggers at Tobias and the girl crouched, shivering on the counter. He makes his way awkwardly skirting the pools of liquid excrement, towards them, hesitant, while continuing to converse on the phone.

Tobias turns his head as the opening of the elevator doors attracts his attention. Charles Wren emerges, ogles at the two cattle munching food in the central area of the atrium, then he sees liquid dung spread all over the famous sunset carpet. He storms towards Tobias, stopping short at the sight of Janet crouched on the desk's surface. "Peabody, what the bloody hell is going on here?"

"Explained to you over the phone, Charles Wren," booms Tobias, "clear enough. I bet you still puzzling how to be keeping your cake and be eatin it? Well I got them cattle eatin' cake yonder okay, but as for keepin' it, don't reckon that'll be the case as you can see, and smell."

"You'll answer for this Tobias Peabody. Very likely in court!" snarls Wren.

"Pity Jack Martin ain't yet here yet filming this for newspapers and prosperity, eh? I did send for him."

"Newspapers? Prosperity? What on Earth are you babbling about?" shouts a confused Charles Wren.

"Nothing, 'cept I got my boy David calling the local *Gazette* right now on his mobile, telling them we got something going on here at this here place and they should send over one of their reporter fellahs."

"Now look here–" Wren gurgles, waving his arms about in fury.

"Seeing you all puffed up and red in the face like that, Charles Wren. You best keep calm or else you be in some danger of your heart seizin' up. Be in need of one of those pace-maker things, you not careful."

Wren, unable to muster an apt response, splutters and, in a mad moment, slaps the counter with an open palm. "I demand that you stop this, this invasion immediately… " He whirls round as a stentorian voice from behind them booms out.

"Mister Wren, what is the meaning of this, this outrage. Those animals, whose are they, and what are they doing in here, our premises? This is intolerable. Explain! Now!"

Janet, still perched on the counter, explains to Tobias, "That is Mr Potteridge, he is our CEO."

"My God," shouts a pin-suited Potteridge, "is that… what I think it is?" he points a wavering finger at the steaming excrement on the carpet. "And this, this… awful, horrible smell. Ugh!"

"Pongs right enough," agrees Tobias, rounding the desk, putting out a hand. "I'm Tobias Peabody."

"Er, Nigel Q. Potteridge. Are these animals yours?" he takes Tobias' hand limply.

"They are sure enough. So, you be the boss-man, eh?" states Tobias.

"I am the CEO of G.E.M.Pix, yes," responds Nigel Potteridge, head up, chin out.

"Don't seem right-headed to me and Mildred, your fellah setting out to cheat us. My good lady, well I gotta say she's been a shadow of herself since we got diddled by your bean counter, Charles Wren here."

"Diddled? We do not diddle Mr Peabody," says Potteridge.

"You do just that. You got something of an arrogant fellah involved in the money side of your business. It takes but one look at him, look, arms going like a windmill, all of a flap, to know he ain't at all with it. P'raps your Mr Wren ain't going about things in a proper, professional manner?"

"Don't be ridiculous. All our employees act with propriety and honesty, and they all have degrees."

"Degrees of takin' advantage of our straightforward country minds more like. You see this here cheque?" Tobias tugs out a crumpled cheque from his shirt pocket, he waves it in the air.

"Yeeess?" Potteridge cautiously peers at the cheque.

"Shoulda had written on it, six thousand pounds, not one hundred, eighty," barks Tobias.

"Really! Explain how one of our accountants made such an enormous discrepancy?" asks Potteridge.

"Meanin' right now?"

"I certainly do mean right now."

Tobias waves away the edgy security man and beckons to Jonathan, standing near the desk. "Son, I now think we best calm the cattle down some. 'Nother bag of feed-cake in the Land Rover." Jonathan nods, and strides out of the building to collect more feed for the two animals – still swishing tails, swinging heads left and right, thinking what to do next in this boxy, waterless, barn.

"Now Mr Pottering–"

"Potteridge!" corrects the great man.

"Yep. As I was sayin'. We got two pedigree highland cattle inside this here hallway and three more in the cattle wagon sat outside. We here to make up for a lack of proper filming by your people when they came out to our farm, and we agreed a price for. Your fellahs had free run of my magnificent pedigree herd for two days, for the special filming of. So when we get a cheque in the post for a miserable one hundred and eighty pounds instead of six grand we expected, I said to my blessed lady we gotta take the herd, well five of 'em, to Exeter, to Charles Wren's town office, so he and Jack Martin can film them all over again. Then I reckon we get paid in full. That's why we are here Mr Porridge, to get the filming done proper and get paid proper, as agreed."

"It's Potteridge," Potteridge says, despairingly.

"Whatever."

"Excuse me," says Potteridge as he backs away from Tobias. "I must speak to Mr Wren privately."

"You do that," Tobias mutters, barely audible in the mounting ruckus.

"Mr Wren," Potteridge thunders. "Over here!"

Tobias' Cattle

Charles Wren, with foreboding, scuttles to a cleanish corner of the atrium where Mr Potteridge is pointing.

Tobias watches them huddled together, he smiles at Wren's magnificent gesticulations in support of a one-sided explanation of the negotiations at the farm between the film crew, himself, Tobias and Mildred.

The security man, Stephen, comes over, growling at Tobias, "See here Mr Peabody, you will move them cattle out of here, right now, and stop that man spreading corn or whatever all over the place. I've already telephoned the police, and if necessary I shall call the fire brigade."

Tobias says, "Suit yourself, we'll be outa here soon as your top fellahs are agreeable to settling for services rendered."

"D'you hear me?" hisses the security man, shaking a fist. "I said, I want you gone. Now–"

"Disturbin' ain't it," interrupts Tobias, looking across at Janet. "Lack of respect nowadays. Nobody doing what they should, polite like, while others doing what they shouldn't. What we gonna do about it, I ask?"

"Now you look here–" starts Stephen straightening up, puffing out his chest aggressively.

Tobias angles his head conspiratorially and beckons him to come closer. Puzzled, Stephen does so. Tobias single-handed, grasps Stephen's uniform by the shirt collar, hoists him onto tip-toe, saying, "You need get some launderin' done to this smart outfit you wearin'. D'you know why?"

An almost dangling Stephen, barely able to shake his head, asks, "W-w-why?" he blurts out.

Tobias moon-walks the man backwards into the slurry spread over the sunrise carpet, "Because it's got cow shit all over it, that's why," then, with his steel-strong arm, forces Stephen down on to his knees. "There, see what I mean? You gotta learn cattle don't know different when it comes to bein' unpleasant, but we two-legged, upright folk, we should be civilised... an' polite. What you say to that?"

"Mr Peabody," says Potteridge, coming over, hands in dive posture, thus separating the two combatants. "I want this matter cleared up, now. Wren says you–"

Tobias drops Stephen to accommodate the boss man. He says, "No disputing cow shit spread all over that fine, fine carpet of yours. I dunno 'bout clearing it up, can set real hard, like my Mildred's burnt pancakes."

"I mean, the matter of the payment, not, er, the mess."

"Well now," Tobias beckons Wren over. "Best your Mr Pottering gets to hear what we agreed, eh?"

Wren sidles alongside Potteridge while the security man, Stephen, trousers dripping with cow muck, spreads his arms in despair and waddles away.

Janet, still crouched on the desk's top, warily eyes the two creatures, as if out of a horror movie, waving their heads, and snorting and sniffing for more cattle feed. Then a smiling Jonathan, having finished dispensing more feed for the animals, comes alongside Janet, drops the empty hessian sack on the counter, opens his arms wide to scoop and lift her gently down from the counter. She smooths her skirt, whispers a breathless, "Oh, thank you." Janet admires this country adonis with his blue eyes, tanned, corded arms and curly brown hair. Oh yes. Now focus my dear on your job. Job? What the devil can I do about it? She smiles at Jonathan as she picks up the phone to call Belinda. She asks Wren's secretary for a teeny-weeny favour. She listens, nods and places the receiver on its rest, returns her attention to this young, country gentleman stood in front of her. This is not the boy-meets-girls scenario she'd envisaged. To hell with cows. But… ah, about these darned cows? "Are you with Mr Peabody?" she inquires sweetly.

"Sure am lady, youngest son. Here to give Pa a hand with his troubles," he looks at the name tag hanging from a cord round her neck. "Janet Morgan."

Janet realizes she is clutching a well-muscled weatherbeaten forearm. He pats her hand firmly. "Very nice to meet you, Janet," he says politely, bending down to pick up and hand her high-heeled shoes.

"Thank you, Mr Peabody–"

"It's Jonathan. Now 'scuse me I gotta go." A renewed snorting takes his mind off Janet's shapely legs as she attempts, elegantly, to pull on her shoes. "Dang me if Dorothy's sister's got one of your fancy wall hangings stuck on a horn. Hey lady, you got any matadors hereabouts?" he grins wide, then laughs out loud.

Wren is speaking urgently to Potteridge, "I made Mr Peabody a fair offer, based on our corporate scale of payments, to cover the filming of his highland cattle for the stampede scene, number thirty-three, for the, at present untitled, movie. It was agreed we would settle on a per head basis. This came to–"

A tearing, ripping sound echoes within the atrium

as Dorothy's sister shakes her head trying to get the canvas wall-hanging from covering her eyes. Snort, snort as she scythes her horns this way and that.

Tobias, impartial to the beasts' wrecking of the establishment, says, "First, we got to tell about our other negotiatin' situation. Did you tell your boss man all about that, Charles Wren?"

Wren presses on, ignoring Tobias, "We came to the decision that G.E.M.Pix would pay Mr Peabody to film a highland cattle scene at a per-head rate, instead of a day rate, for one hundred and eighty pounds."

"A head rate instead of a one-off payment seems fair enough to me," says Potteridge. "Although I have to say those are wildly differing figures you both bandy about, one hundred and eighty as against six thousand pounds?"

"Gotta say we offered your filmin' fellahs the run of the place and full access to the herd for as many days as they wanted, also plenty food and drink, sleepin' place on offer too. It mounted to six grand which your Charles Wren thought as being a good bargain. So we signed on that figure," he looks hard at Wren. "Gotta say your man took a real tough line with me, 'bit like negotiatin' with them top money-men in the city. Me, well it was embarrassing' when he said that of me too. Me bein' a poor illiterate farmer like."

"Spare us the tear-jerk... " cries Charles Wren.

"If six thousand is the figure you agreed to Wren, how came you paid this man only one-eighty?"

"Your Mr Wren's not tellin' you the whole story," says Tobias. "The truth is that he somehow lost the paper we signed. I do reckon, cross-me-heart, that it was stolen at the Shoulder of Mutton in our village, during a celebratory pint at the bar, along with his attaché case. But your Mr Wren here, he being too much of a gentleman to admit such. We sure got some bad people out in the countryside. Local man, Constable Wells, he's looking into it."

Wren's mouth drops and his eyes goggle at this outrageous lie, "Mr Peabody is straying from the facts of the matter, sir. So do please listen to me. First this so-called highland herd is only twelve stro–"

"Next thing you be saying," interrupts Tobias, "is we spun a coin to agree what you be paying us?"

Charles Wren's mouth rat-traps shuts. He drops a gesticulating hand by his side. This tell-tale move is not missed by Tobias.

"Very amusing, Peabody," smiles Potteridge. "Now then Wren, what do you say?"

"The police will be here any moment… " Wren starts.

"No, I mean about Mr Peabody's claim to have been, er, cheated?" says Potteridge.

Tobias interrupts, "I reckon at a pinch we can squeeze Dorothy into that elevator lift over there. Then we get to take her all the way up to Mr Wren's posh office, and after that we go locate your den Mr Pottersby."

"What the devil!" exclaims Potteridge, looking over his shoulder as an excess of snorting, ripping and tearing rents the air.

"Dorothy's the bulky one. Spirited gal ain't she?" admires Tobias, glancing at the wrecking scene.

Geriatricks 1

Potteridge's mouth is a-gape at the continuing damage to what was once his proud domain. "Look –!"

"Since we came to persuade your Charles Wren we be right in this matter, I reckon it only proper we be gathering in his office to do the talking, cattle and all," states Tobias. He turns, shouting, "Hey Jonathan. Get that Dorothy movin' toward that elevator lift yonder," he turns back to Potteridge. "Now, I got another three beasts rarin' to go in the cattle wagon parked outside, I'll get my other boy David to bring 'em in just now. Swell the numbers, eh?"

"Good God man, what, what… " stammers a near helpless Potteridge.

"You stumblin' over your words Mr Pollidge, you should watch out for yourself. Mumblin', old age and frustratin' moments can get you placed with one of them there mind fixers."

"Potteridge, it's Potteridge," Potteridge yells. "And, no. You can't go just anywhere you like. I forbid it."

"Seems I'm wastin' me time here," grunts Tobias. "You all talking machines. No bleedin' action."

The security man, Stephen, returns wearing a spotless blue outfit. He places his hands on his hips. "Right that's it. I'm calling the fire brigade," he starts to pull out his mobile phone… then Janet steps before him and lays her hand on his arm. "Don't do that Stephen. The next move is down to me."

"You! What on earth can you do, a mere receptionist?"

Janet shrugs. "Well, you're not doing so very well yourself are you? And it would seem our so-called managers are doing even less well to resolve the situation. So... watch and learn."

He raises an eyebrow as he one-handed folds, disconnecting his mobile. Janet smiles; she reaches under the counter to locate a leather-bound visitors book and a blue folder. She opens the folder, takes up a biro and starts to write. Finally Janet says out loud: "Mr Potteridge, would you come over here, please sir."

"What? Why?" Trying to locate a new voice in the melee.

"I need you to encourage, persuade, Mr Peabody to sign our visitors' book sir."

Mr Potteridge opens and closes his mouth. Wren comes up snarling, "This is bloody ridiculous." Stephen the security man spreads his arms in despair. Charles Wren, frustrated, starts to remonstrate with Stephen over the lack of action to remove the animals. They go into a verbal head-to-head.

Janet lays the visitors' book on the counter, opens it up, saying out loud, "Mr Potteridge?"

He looks over. "I really don't need this Miss Morgan–"

"Please sir." Janet gently takes hold of his wrist, leading him gently round to her side of the counter. She scans his face holding his eyes with hers. "A signature sir – just here," she points down.

'Signature?" Potteridge looks down, puzzled. He sees an open company chequebook lying inside a blue folder. It is filled in and the amount written is six thousand pounds. Potteridge, a gleam of understanding in his eyes, nods, takes a silver fountain pen from his suit top pocket. He asks, "Where did this come from? Our corporate cheque books are not to be found just lying about–"

"I had it sent down from Mr Wren's office, sir," says Janet fluttering her eyelids.

Potteridge grunts, signs the cheque. Janet asks him if Mr Wren would countersign, since two signatures were necessary. Potteridge looks over at Wren who is still rowing with the security man. "I don't think our Mr Wren would be amenable just now."

"But sir? We must have two signatures."

"Our Mr Peabody doesn't know that, does he?" Potteridge retorts.

Janet looks at him. He shakes his head severely. She quietly tears the signed cheque from the cheque book gesturing for Tobias to come over to the desk. Janet proffers the cheque. Tobias looks at it, smiles and grins, then pockets it.

"Now Mr Peabody, if you will be kind enough to sign here. She points with the pen to a slip of paper lying on the visitors' book, it is a receipt for six thousand pounds.

Tobias looks at Potteridge, who nods, then at Janet, who nods. He scrawls an indecipherable mark.

Janet puts the folder away, makes a notation in the visitors' book, and smiles brightly at the two men. "That is all gentlemen, thank you very much."

Tobias loudly proclaims, "By God, we been in this here place too bloody long, gettin' ourselves into a bunch of wordage an' such. Jonathan, get them cattle rounded and loaded up. We're off back to the farm."

Potteridge shouts, "Be off with you and your damned cows. Thank your lucky stars I'm not bringing in both police and the Fire Brigade."

"Eh, eh? What, what?" blusters a bewildered Wren, looking around.

"I'll see you in my office later Wren," barks Potteridge, and to the security man, "you, get the cleaning staff in here straight away and I want that awful, er, mess cleared up. Go on, go, go, go!"

"We makin' off now Charles Wren, " Tobias says. "Sure you don't want us to wait around a mite longer until your Jack Martin gets here to be filmin' my pedigree highland cattle?"

"Err. Nooo." Wren eyes Tobias warily. What the hell is going on, what has the CEO done to persuade this oaf, his sons and their awful beasts to quit the place? He is bemused, and relieved, as he watches the Peabody boys whip and herd the two smashing and crashing highland cows through the building's doorway into the open air.

Tobias laughs out loud, "Just when they gettin' settled in too." He circles behind the reception counter to come up close to Janet, places one gnarled hand gently on her shoulder. "You got my sincere thanks Miss Janet. You are some girl y'know. You be invited to my farm anytime. I'd be right pleased to be introducing you to my breedin' stock, an' I'm talking bi-peds here – a very 'andsome one in particular." Janet blushes, lowers her eyes demurely, pops her pink hanky into her handbag and, oddly, feels the urge to curtsey.

Tobias continues: "But don't you go a-frettin', we

country gentlemen know how to treat ladies proper, as well we got whole lot of entertaining going on out there in Loughton village, skittles in the pub getting popular now we're in the county league; and dancing at the village hall. Our Jonathan, he keen on a dance or two. Do you dance Janet?"

She, interested, smiles, nodding, "I do like country dancing, and sometimes we have line-dancing here in the Town Hall. Are you familiar with Line Dancing Mr–"

"Yep. We get into that Yankee prancin' at our village hall. Hard wood floor, jest the right kinda floorin' for a roisterous knees-up, so no fancy hob-nail boots. Me and Mildred go there regular. We know all 'em Line Dance routines, and best of 'em all – Honky Tonky Highway'. A right enjoyable evening, to end a month's hard slog."

"You have live band?" she asks.

"Sure do. A trio: Cornish singin' lady, a geetar strummer, plays the accordion too, and a ginger-haired young fellah just startin' out, whacking hell out of a pair o' drums. Lotta young ladies getting there these days from close-by villages, Guess our farm boys attractin' them, as well as the dancin'. We get both old folk and young folk. But when it gets down to the fancy steps, we oldies got the footfall the youngsters ain't yet got to match. We get good behaviour mostly. Okay, I see some dating and smooching on the balcony from time to time, and I can't, daren't, say what goes on in close-by Haymaker's Spinney. Nuff said, eh?"

"This Loughton village sounds like a very exciting place," says Janet.

He smiles, straightening-up. "Leastwise last

Tobias' Cattle

Saturday of the month it be. Now lass, let me write sommat in yon visitor book," Tobias leans over, takes up her pen, writes down a number. "That does it for now, and thank you Janet Morgan."

Janet looks at what Tobias has written, "A telephone number?"

"Jonathan: steady, shy man, heart of gold and he be real assiduous with his farming methods. But contrarily, he's none too clever at contacting girls – but t'otherway round, who's to say who calls who?"

"Oh, you old devil, Mr Peabody."

'Meanwhile lady, I got me some cattle to take on home..."

* * *

Outside Jonathan and David round up the two beasts slurping water at the nearby fountain, to chase them up the ramp into the cattle wagon. They start securing the back-slats while Tobias relaxes and leans casually against the bonnet of the pick up munching on a beef sandwich and sipping cider. His eyes brighten when he sees a familiar SUV draw alongside. Out leaps Jack Martin and Fuzzy Ito. The wide grinning Ito, attired in a blue jacket, gold waistcoat, shorts and sandals, immediately focuses his camera on the two toiling brothers and the shaking, rattling cattle wagon, while Jack, clad in a leather jacket and blue denims, strides over to greet and shake hands with Tobias.

"Good to see you Mr Peabody. We've been called here to film some sort of on-going action. According to

Janet it involves yourselves and live cattle. Tell me, what *is* going on?"

Tobias says, "We been settled. Look," He waves the cheque in front of Jack. "All done... hunky-dory!"

Jack looks at the cheque, saying, "Well, good news indeed Tobias," he peers closer, "However, I believe you need a second signature on that cheque, otherwise–"

"Otherwise? What d'you mean, otherwise?" Tobias swigs another mouthful of cider.

"Company cheques need two authorising signatures. Must've been an oversight on the CEO's part. Let me co-sign it, then it'll be valid for payment," Jack suggests.

"Dang me! Thank you Jack," says Tobias. Jack produces a pen, leans his elbows on the vehicle's bonnet to counter-sign the cheque.

Fuzzy Ito comes over to them, camera in hand, "Gleetings. Good you bring highrand crattle here for boss man to see. Eh?"

"Yep! We brung 'em direct, better than Park 'n' Ride, to let them see first hand what magnificent beasts they got in your film. But you be a mite late to get pictures of the action Fritzy. Still and all, you maybe get summat off those CeeCee TV cameras inside. There again you ought to wait awhile until they've cleaned up some, these high-spirited pedigree highland cattle of mine really messed up your reception place, lack of litter see. An' there's quite a pong lingerin' in the air," he chuckles, "maybe a reminder not to be smart with us country folk," Tobias taps the side of his nose. "Know what I mean?"

"Yes I do, and you obviously got to meet our Mr Wren?" asks Jack.

"Sure we met him. He be in there now muckraking. But y'know, he's got no herding ability, be useless down on the farm."

"I doubt he has any ambition to become a farmer, Tobias," says Jack. "But I'm sure he'll remember your visit today. Well, we'll take your advice and return to our studio. We have a feature to put together for an agricultural company, would you believe!" He shakes Tobias' hand and moves toward his SUV.

Ito nods, grins wide, "Grad to meet you 'gain mister Pobody," Tobias grimaces, but gives a thumbs-up.

"Afore you get goin' Jack." Tobias gestures for a puzzled Jack to return alongside him.

"Yeees?" cautious.

They prick up their ears. In the background they hear sirens whoo-whooing, *speeding police cars?*

Tobias theatrically tunnels a hand alongside his mouth, "Got me hearing about investors in films get a percent of the makings–"

"Profit, Tobias, profit," repeats Jack.

"Well, we kind of, we gotta be investors I reckon, by now. So I got to thinkin'... "

"No, we're not going down that road my good friend. Forget it!" Jack raises two hands.

Tobias plunges his hand into his trouser pocket, rattles coins. "How bout we toss for it, Jack?"

Jack stands back, laughing out loud. "You do take the cake... and eat it too.

"Talkin' of cake, them steers getting restless, wanting their feed. So we be takin' our leave of you Jack Martin. You get wind of any profit, you know where we be?"

"You'd best climb into that jalopy of yours..." Jack nods at Tobias' mud-streaked pick up "and get going while you've got the chance. Those sirens don't sound too far away,"

"That be no jalopy Jack, that's a near-new 1952 model, rare as hen's teeth."

A laugh from Jack as he beckons Ito to get into their four-by-four. As they drive away a blue and yellow patrol car bounces over the kerb, narrowly missing a bollard, another skids alongside. Policemen and women leap out and surround the cattle truck and Tobias' Land Rover. Jonathan, David and Tobias, arms high, legs spread wide, take up a mock surrender mode. Soon all three are being patted down in front of a gathering street crowd, camera phones flashing along with shouts and jeers.

The IC Sergeant demands to know why these, he points at the farm vehicles, are trespassing on the town's most famous, and ancient cobbled area.

"Well, it be like this," begins Tobias, "we got an okay from these filmin' folk," he thumbs the building behind him, "they making a film with an old-fashion market town scene. We providin' the er, props they calls 'em, for some fifty pound an hour–"

The Sergeant queries, nodding at the mooing noises coming from the cattle wagon, "With live cattle?"

The WPC alongside, sniffs, "Live all right," she writes down the vehicle's plate details in her notebook.

"Yep, we told be realistic as possible," beams Tobias.

The sergeant shakes his head in wonder, "Who is in charge of this local filming?"

Tobias' Cattle

"You go right on through those automatic doors. Inside is fellah name of Charles Wren, he be in charge."

The Sergeant, poised to leap into action, is arrested by Tobias' hand. "Careful sir," he admonishes.

"Look officer, we gotta get moving. These pedigree animals are acting up, been out of their meadow since early morning, pining for open space, fresh air and decent feed. If they break loose, well heaven only knows what havoc they might cause in the High Street, an' you wouldn't want to see those town folk panicking, yelling and whatnot," says Tobias.

The Sergeant nods, angles his head for them to move off of the cobbled area. He waves for his troops to stand down while he and his colleague head for the automatic double-doored entrance to G.E.M.Pix

Tobias motions his boys to mount up and be off. He climbs into the pick up, signals politely to the police standing there to move aside, and drives onto the road. He follows the cattle truck – out of town!

* * *

Tobias clumps into the kitchen. "Bless me Mildred if I ain't all but all done in. Haymaking's bloody hard work. Could have done with Jonathan helpin' us out. When's he coming back?"

"We got a posh hand-delivered letter from them G.E.M.Pix people."

"Hah, thought we'd done with them and all by now. Hand delivered? You mean by the postie?"

"No, we got company, they brung the letter, they're in the sittin' room," She gestures, a sweep of her hand.

"Who'm that be?" asks Tobias.

"Jonathan!" says Mildred excitedly. "Our Jonathan."

"Well, he ain't no visitor."

A yell... Jonathan's voice, "In here, Pa!"

Tobias grumbles his way to the door, stops, "Bless my socks. I do say a big helloooo, Janet, Janet Morgan."

Dressed in tan pleated skirt and a floral cream blouse, Janet approaches Tobias. "Mr Peabody, it is so nice to meet you again. We are sorry we kept our liaison from you and Mrs Peabody, but after that trouble at G.E.M.Pix, Jonathan and I started to meet discreetly at the dances at the Loughton Village hall."

"We been making out, Pa," says Jonathan proudly, "a couple of months now. We got good news... "

Janet takes Tobias' head in both hands and kisses him full on the lips "... GrandPa!"

Tobias slumps into an armchair, "Dang me, friggin' surprises all round seems like, these days."

"Got 'nother surprise for you here, husband." Mildred hands over a letter. 'Postie just brought it."

Tobias looks at the logo stamp: 'G.E.M.Pix'. He flip-flaps it against his palm.

"Well, open it. Let's see what it is," says Mildred.

"Don't rush me woman," Tobias rips open the envelope, pulls out a letter with a compliment slip stapled to it. He says, "What be this then?"

Mildred comes over, "Maybe they wantin' their money back."

"Lemme read it." Tobias slips on his reading glasses,

peers at the letter. "They do too! Well bugger me! They billin' us for six thousand pounds," he reads out the words, "For cleaning, carpeting and wall hanging at UAPS atrium, whatever that be. Materials and labour, six thousand pounds, for God's Sake."

Mildred says, "You'd better up sticks and beetle down there and sort 'em out, like last time? Heh, heh!"

"Jonathan, what be this piece of paper stapled to this bill?"

Jonathan rises, come across, looks at the papers Tobias is waving about. "That's a compliment slip Pa, its got a G.E.M.Pix logo and Charles Wren's name printed over it. There's a hand-written something..."

"Charles Wren, eh? So what's he wrote?"

"Couple of words Pa: 'Last Laugh'.

"The man's a bloody idiot, I do say. Pass me that other letter that you brung along."

Jonathan gives it to Tobias. He flips open the unsealed plain envelope, shucking out a colourful card. "Well if it ain't an invitation to meet producer, director and actin' folk at a film preview, which they say got scenes showing our highland cattle. Dang me."

"Oooh, that'll be worth going and seeing then. Where is it, Tobias?"

"Their studio near Craxton, 15th August. Says they putting out wine and food before showin' the film."

"What's it called Tobias," she urges, "this picture?"

"Aaaah, let's see, Yeah, they calling it: '*Highland Hijack*'.

A ROTARY RENDEZVOUS

Rotary clubs, for the benefit of all, so frequently they do meet,
With clockwork regularity, yearly, monthly, weekly ... to greet.
Nowadays even clubs profiled geriatric, remain so very strong,
Do note, a number of members have been with them all along.
Always toiling for community benefit both locally and overseas,
Rotary fame is spread far and wide fighting poverty and disease.
Members arrive on foot, bike and car to be at their usual venue,
Before lunch they relax, glasses in hand ... friendships to renew.
To articulate on policies, weather, with aging health uppermost,
JL's immobility is massaged daily by chiropractor, he does boast.
FI's sixteen trips to the bathroom overnight is greeted with awe,
HIL's aerobic activities bring the house down, so they all guffaw.
QT declares his cricket injury is due to an irregular ball-bounce,
A's shopping trolley toe-injury? In court, that firm he'll trounce.
LL pipes up, 'Aliens landed in my garden, and no I wasn't blotto,

Geriatricks 1

It was mister and missus Cyborg dropped in from Rotary Ploto'.

Then, their admirable speaker arrives with an enthusiastic wave,
President greets and treats his guest at the bar, he's so very brave.
He orders drinks, 'Mine's a vodka-martini, shaken not shtirred',
'Our chap's gone balmy, he thinks he's Julius Caesar,' is the word.
Top-dog secretary gesticulates, lunch is a-ready, lets go and dine,
The seated strive to rise, old bones creak, 'Oh, aid us to the wine'.
Zimmer frame, walking cane, there is no moan, groan or scowl,
'We shall get to that dining table, hook or by crook,' they growl.
All now assembled under President's tranquil gaze they do wait.
His Majesty rings the bell, then a pause for their banter to abate.
Meanwhile he discreetly checks for their dress-code compliance,
He discerns no rings in nose, lips or eyebrow, nor any ordnance.
President welcomes speaker, guests, members and two in a daze,
Then Grace with aplomb and dignity, 'Rotary ways' … as always.

A Rotary Rendezvous

All seated, the kitty-box goes round, ah, better than Robin's bow,
Ladies, gents, guests, age before beauty, to the buffet go tally-ho.

All tuck in, luscious food, hunger assuaged they communicate,
Dodgy weather, cranky neighbours, web? These to be our fate?
Vice P nudges Pres from his trance, 'Waken up, get a move on,'
Pres's tremulous voice proclaims: 'Fee, fi, fooo ... oh, it's gone',
He scans his script, 'Legss stretch, all rise, we must now toast,'
Glasses raised high, all sing, 'The Queen', loyalty they do post,
Top table's now a-buzz, Hons' Treas and Sec so lead the posse,
Kitty box is declared, yes, its enough to finance a seaside cossy.
Sec, 'Our speaker next week by popular demand, is Mr I. Soar,
Hang gliding for the elderly. Sponsors, to help us aid the poor.
So come ye all and sign up, guaranteed it will be a super sight,'
Enthusiasm knows no bounds, hands hoist high for this flight.
Upstanding now, Pres plays the Ace in his hand, showbiz time.

Geriatricks 1

He intros speaker Cecil, who does cometh from a wetter clime.
Rapturous clapping greets a long-anticipated speaker, to hear,
'From Devon I hail it ought be known, all the way in top gear,'

'My talk today is on the Bucket, a product famed thru history,
This pre-pipe utensil so vital, it... ' Cecil warms to his oratory,
'...is made of plaited cane, tin, bronze even up-market chrome,
To give you a handle on this... it is a symbol of ancient Rome,'
At this catcalls resound, Pres leaps to his feet and raises a hand,
'You, you, you, any more of this and you're exiled to Legoland,'
Assertive Cecil continues his rivetting eulogy in voice to thrill,
'Isaac Newton did define, water so contained... would not spill,'
Wolf-whistles abound, Pres leaps to his feet and he does swoop,
'Hey, you HH, you're in line to do a hang glider loopa-de-loop,'
'Now he thinks he's Pontius Pilate,' bemoans Sec, 'so save us all,'
VP grunts, 'Its his magnetic personality, he hails from Southall,'

A Rotary Rendezvous

Cecil's monologue goes on, 'Inventing a bucket was so brilliant,
So beyond the pale... also those made of leather are so resilient,'
Speaker poses the question, 'how does the modern bucket fare?
Well, sales are up this year, fourteen alone to northern Abedare.'

Its true to say some older members find it hard to concentrate,
Eyelids a-droop, heads nod, a somnolent snore, we must relate.
Speaker marches on, 'In an emergency, it can be used as a sink.'
At this amazing revelation, those at top table are tickled pink,
'All-purpose too, turn it upside down, it can be used as a seat,
The humble bucket has dozens of uses that are so hard to beat,
Now for stir-frying, cut it in half, you've got yourselves a wok,
It is well-known that Chinese cafeterias keep dozens in stock,'
Sec whispers, 'Pour him another glass, we got to shut him up,'
Pres, 'I told you weeks ago this would be a load of codswallup,'
Cecil goes on, 'The bedrock of our society, the mighty bucket,

All round the world, Crewe to Cairo, Nan-ching to Nantucket,
Also down on the farm... two at a time with a shoulder frame,'
'Oh the yoke's on us,' hisses Sec, 'slip him a double of the same,'
'In cities and towns you see buckets being used as flower pots,
Some decorated with fleur-de-lys! They are lilies tied in knots.'

Treas now queries, 'Can they be musical, used as a Tom-Tom?'
Cecil, po-faced, 'And what rustic outback did you come from?
Ahem! I've strayed beyond my alloted time, I am rather afraid,
Hic! I must wind up and take my leave, I must not be delayed,'
A vote of thanks is now due: Pres, 'Not you H, I'll go with FJJ.'
FJJ warms up, 'That you've educated us all, I am bound to say,
Your wisdom on the usage of the pail, held us all in your sway,
Ne'er again shall we utter, KK kicked the bucket just yesterday.
Your expertise is second to none, your knowledge formidable,'
Cecil delights in this, he creates a warm smile, all so agreeable.

A Rotary Rendezvous

Grunts of approval greet FJJ's pearls of wisdom, as he finalises,
Raucous applause has Cecil bowing...until he almost capsizes.
A final word rolls of Pres's tongue: 'We will surely never forget.
The mighty bucket, and your talk today was one prized nugget.
So we will always be inspired, and our club will forever boast,
Cecil was here this day! Now, please all rise for the final toast.'